SPIRIT OF GONZALES

Betsy Wagner

Spirit of Gonzales
©2019 Betsy Wagner

Betsy Wagner
P.O. Box 171145
San Antonio, Texas 78217

spiritofgonzales@att.net
https://spiritofgonzales.com

713-819-5599

ISBN: 978-0-578-43880-1

SPIRIT OF GONZALES

Timeline for the Life of Sydnie Gaston Kellogg

Part 1

Life Before Texas

1

October 1819 – Cleaning out the Tailor Shop in Cincinnati

Tweet, tweet! The shrill whistle of the Cincinnati Street Police sounded.

I was very young, but I do recall the sound of that whistle. I probably think I remember the rest because it was told to me so many times.

"Stop," the policeman said as he put out his hand to halt the carriages coming up Broadway.

Neigh, bang! Another horse slammed into the two carriages already blocking the cobbled roadway.

"Are you hurt, ma'am?" The policeman knelt down by our mama. There was no reply. He blew his whistle again and called for help.

"Oh, Mama." I cried as I knelt by Mama lying crumpled in the street. I stood with my hands out. They said I clasped my hands together and cried for Mama, as if I was afraid to touch her.

Apparently, it was such a scene a crowd gathered. That was when we first saw Mr. George Davis. He was very tall and so underweight he might have been described as skeletal. He lifted me up and carried me out of harm's way.

I continued to cry for my mama, and the tall man consoled me. "There, now, she'll be okay. Where is your Daddy?"

"He's gone." That was all I could say.

Then my sister Susie explained. "Our daddy died."

Mr. Davis turned around and saw Susie peering up at him from inside a blue wool bonnet lined with white fur. Susie was holding our little brother that day, and John was shivering in her arms.

"Mama was moving his things." She pointed to a shop behind them. The sign in the front window read GASTON TAILOR.

The narrow walkway was piled up with boxes and bundles of fabric waiting to be loaded into the Gaston carriage. Mama and her friend Cheryl Knox were trying to load them when a horse bolted and knocked Mama down.

The tall, skeletal man was George Washington Davis, who had recently arrived in Cincinnati. He rented a room above our daddy's tailor shop. Everyone in the neighborhood knew of our daddy's recent death, and Mr. Davis was vaguely aware of our circumstances. Now he was involved.

Mama's friend Cheryl Knox was known for being a bit dramatic. "Oh, Susie, whatever shall we do?" Mrs. Knox stood wringing her hands in total, clueless abandon. She lingered with a long, hopeless look at Mr. Davis.

"I'll help you," he said. And that was all it took. That was when Mr. George Davis took charge.

George handed me over to Mrs. Knox and asked her to step back. He packed the boxes and bundles into the two carriages. By the time he finished, Mama was revived and seated in her own carriage. Mrs. Knox helped me get into her carriage. Susie got in with little John, and we were all set.

"Show me the way," George said. He drove Mama's carriage and followed Mrs. Knox to our home.

December 1819 – Making Popcorn

There's also the story of the first time Mr. Davis came for a visit with us. It was on a workday in December, and we wanted to have some holiday fun. I remember this story so well, I can tell it perfectly, even though Mama says I was so young I couldn't possibly remember—I've just heard it so often it seems like a real memory. Mama had just said good bye to the last few customers.

"Are they gone?" Susie asked.

"Yes, they're gone." Mama smiled as she turned her back to the heavy door and pushed it closed. "And now we'll string some popcorn." She clapped her hands and reached down for me. "I'll bring Sydna, and you go get your brother."

Susie dashed away. "Little John...." Her voice faded down the hall.

On most days, I think our home was a regular open house. Ladies came from all over Cincinnati wanting Mama to help them pretty-up their homes. The rooms of our home were crowded with the work Mama continued after Daddy Gaston died. The place was packed in every corner with stacks of fabric, baskets of trims, and unfinished projects. Every day Mama made somebody happy with her talents. But when business was over and the ladies were gone, we could have precious family time.

Mama said she took me into the kitchen and sat me up on the table just in reach of the cupboard.

They said I had chubby little arms, and that I stretched them as far as I could to grab a jar full of hard yellow seeds. We were going to make our traditional popcorn. I tucked the jar into a big pocket on the front of my smock. Mama took an orange and was just cutting it when we all heard the knock at the door.

As the story goes, Susie was just bringing little John into the kitchen when she heard that knock. Her eyes flashed at Mama, and she protested because it was after working hours.

But Mama said, "I'll only be a minute. Put little John down and give him some of that orange."

Mama went to answer the door, and while she was gone John took a bit of orange between his two little fingers and placed it on his tongue. He closed his eyes and puckered a bit as the citrus oozed down his throat. John always loved oranges, and it tickled us to watch his reaction to the sourness.

I guess we were quiet, just listening for Mama to come back to the kitchen. We listened for her footsteps, but instead we heard her laughing, and we heard a man's voice.

Then we heard Mama calling us. "Sydnie, Susie. Bring little John into the parlor."

Susie gave little John another bit of orange and bundled him into her arms. I do remember that I clutched at my sister's soft woolen skirt and I shuffled alongside her into the front room. I remember the scent of spruce. When Susie stopped, they said I peeked out from behind Susie's dress. There was a tall man pulling a gray hat between his long, slender thumb and forefinger in a nervous fidget. I must have peered upward, finally looking into his face. I remember his cheekbones were sharp, covered with a thin layer of ruddy skin.

"Children, you remember my friend, Mr. Davis," Mama said. "He's come to visit us. And look, he brought us a Christmas tree."

A young spruce stood next to him.

"Hello, children," he said, and Susie shook his hand.

I tucked myself back into Susie's skirt, and I'm sure I wanted to touch those green needles.

I must have recognized him. Maybe it was just that Mama had mentioned him. Mrs. Knox came to stay with us those days so Mama could go out sometime. But this was the first time Mr. Davis came to visit us in our home.

Then Mama told him, "We were just going to pop some corn, George. Will you join us?" Mama motioned for us to go in front of the fireplace.

He sat the small tree in its pot on a corner table and offered to help us with the popcorn.

Mama took the wire basket from the hearth. She sprinkled the kernels to make a sparse layer in the bottom of the basket. Mr. Davis took the handle from her and held it into the flames. In awkward silence we all stood, just waiting. I closed my eyes and took in the aroma of the Christmas season. Soon the sound of little explosions broke the silence.

"Ooh." Little John rounded his lips, and his eyes grew big. He clapped his hands. Susie took a seat on the sofa and snuggled our little brother in her lap. Feeling exposed from behind Susie's skirt, I sucked in my cheeks and stood with my hands behind my back. I think I did that a lot in those years.

Mama dashed away to get the molasses. She came back with a large dish and a jar of thick, brown, gooey sweetness.

Mr. Davis brought the wire basket out of the fire and turned to face us. He stood full height, so the basket passed above my head. The toasty smell of fresh popcorn was especially good in the room that night. Mama put the large dish on the table, and Mr. Davis dumped all the soft, white bits of corn onto it.

Then Mama explained our holiday celebration. "We have a tradition, George. We string and eat in celebration of the holiday." Mama dipped a wooden spoon into the jar, pulled it out, and drizzled molasses over the hot popped corn.

Susie took one tiny morsel and put it to our brother's lips.

"We'll eat this batch," Mama continued, "and pop another for stringing. George, please bring everyone a napkin from that drawer in the sideboard."

"Yes, dear," he replied.

Dear? Susie remembered thinking, *Did he call our mama dear?*

I propped my elbows on the table and interlocked my fingers. I sucked in my cheeks and watched Mr. Davis.

He pulled out a chair for Susie and handed her a napkin. A gentle smile crept onto his face as he noticed a bit of molasses slipping out the side of John's mouth. Mama wiped the goo away and introduced each of us by name.

"This is my son, John, and my oldest daughter, Susie."

Mr. Davis smiled and bowed a bit. He pulled out a second chair and Mama sat down by Susie. "And who have we over here?" he asked as he came toward me.

"This is our Sydnie. We call her Sydna or just Syd." Mama patted my hand because she knew I was nervous. "Sometimes she's shy."

"Sydnie." He repeated my name and patted my head. Then he pulled out a chair to sit next to me.

Mr. Davis passed me the plate, and I took a glob of white-and-brown goo. I remembered those long fingers, and how they had rescued me from the street on that horrible moving day.

"Rebecca, you have lovely children," he said. "I hope we can all be friends." He looked at me and I gave him my best smile.

This was our formal introduction to the man who would become our Daddy D. Within a year, we became the fortunate children of George Washington Davis on the occasion of his marriage to our mama in October 1820. Our first winter together in Cincinnati was as sweet as drizzled popcorn, and then came the spring. Mama wanted to be near her family. She had a brother Thomas who raised horses in Kentucky. Daddy D. wanted Mama to be happy. In the summer of 1821, George packed the house and moved us all to Kentucky where the race horses lived.

August 1821 – Green River, Kentucky

I was four when we moved to Kentucky, and my brother John was almost three. Daddy bought an exceptional lodging house on the main road to the courthouse in Greensburg. It was to be our home for ten years. He hired Jonas Long, who became Daddy's right-hand man.

"Whoa." The clip-clopping of the horses' hooves slowed to a stop in front of the Green River Inn. "Careful now," Jonas said as he reached out to the newly arriving boarders, helping them down from their carriage. "Step on here, so's yore shoes stays clean," Jonas advised.

"Oh, look, Addie, a step and a paved walk." The adulation started at the carriage step and continued to the front porch where the boarders sat in one of two ornate swings to wait for Jonas to bring their bags.

On Saturdays, John and I sat in one of the swings to watch the parade of guests come and go. We were often mistaken for twins, with teeth too big for our mouths and yellow hair resembling straw. Braids kept mine somewhat under control, but John had a cowlick that made his stick out. Freckles were sprinkled across John's nose, and he had an endearing grin. Our skin was the light brown of diluted sand. Our pale brows and lashes made our eyes stand out like blueberries.

"What adorable children. What is your name, child?" The question became predictable.

Green River Inn

"She's Sydna, but I call her Syd. I'm John," my outgoing little brother told them, pointing his finger for clarity. I was glad to let John speak for me.

Then Mama appeared at the door. "Welcome to Green River Inn." She encouraged her guests to come inside. "Susie will sign you in and give you a room. Our midday meal is at one o'clock, just over there." She motioned with a graceful hand toward the long table in a space beyond the registration desk. "If you wish to join us, please let us know right away." To watch Mama you'd believe that keeping an inn was the most fun a woman could have. If Mama ever had a bad day in Kentucky, I never knew it.

Once the guests came inside, Susie's work began. "Please sign here," she instructed. At a very mature thirteen, she kept the records. Her tranquil smile and long-lashed eyes made it easy for the guests to cooperate. Susie took after Mama with her gift for approachability. I wished I could be like them. Thorough, reliable, they always knew which guests stayed in which rooms. Sometimes Susie rewrote the name in the book just to be sure she could read it.

If anything was ever left behind in a room, Susie made it her business to wrap the missing item in brown paper, write the family name on the paper, and secure the item in the big vault until it could be returned. In the lower right drawer of the big reception desk was a little wooden box. Susie scratched "left behind" on the hinged lid. Inside the box was a set of little white cards where she recorded the missing items and filed them by the owners' names. She had the cards organized from Abbott to Zweigle.

"Good morning, young lady." A handsome and dignified young man introduced himself to Susie. "Morgan is my name. Joshua Morgan." He took his black felt hat off his head as Mama came from the kitchen. "Ma'am." He nodded to her, with the hat over his heart. "I'll be comin' through here now. It's on my circuit.

That is, I'll be conducting burials and marriage ceremonies in this region."

Mama and Susie looked at each other, I guess wondering what to make of him. I couldn't remember ever seeing a preacher before.

He started again. "Well, I was wonderin', ma'am, if we might hold Sabbath worship in your parlor." He motioned around the room and sort of inspected it a bit. "It's really quite a remarkable place." Then he waited for Mama to speak.

"What sort of preaching do you do?" Mama asked.

"I bring a Methodist expression of Christianity, ma'am. I'm in hopes of finding Bible-minded Christians who wish to worship and follow the teachings of Jesus Christ." He gave her a minute to think about that. "I preach from the Holy Scriptures." He held out a well-worn Bible and concluded his simple resume.

"Methodist. It's been a long time," Mama said quietly. Joshua Morgan looked a lot at Susie, as if he was getting an impression of her. After a thoughtful delay, Mama agreed, "Yes, I think that would do us all a lot of good."

Susie assigned the missionary a room, and the next day we held the first of many Sabbath Day services. Our place became the area house of worship.

Mama loved singing and knew most of the words to the hymns. We didn't have a piano, but Reverend Morgan hummed out the first note. While everybody was trying to hit the right tone, he tapped his boot to set a rhythm. Then he sang out the first few words. Eventually the song began, and everyone caught up. Sometimes there was fiddle music, but mostly just voices. It all sits in my memory as a beautiful thing.

"Amazing grace, how sweet the sound." Mama looked up at Daddy D. and their voices blended. Preacher Morgan closed his eyes and crowed out the words, "Come, ye who love the Lord." It went on like that until the minister decided it was time to preach.

Sabbath was one of the many things that made our inn special, and we had plenty of visitors when the preacher came 'round. I came to believe it earned us some favor with the Lord in the years to come.

January 1822 – Finding a Secret Place

Because we were just little ones when we first arrived in Kentucky, John and I played in a protected section of the front parlor. But in a short time we became old enough to take lessons and assume family chores.

S-y-d-n-i-e. I practiced writing my name, and John tried to write his. There was no school in the county, but Susie held classes for us in the early mornings. Mama bought us a school book, *The Bryer New American Spelling Book*. In section four, the spelling lessons taught names with the meaning and origin of each one.

Ann means graceful. Beverly originated from the beaver stream. Carolyn is the feminine form of Charles, and it means a song of happiness. It went on like that through the alphabet. In the J section we learned John means that God is gracious.

"What does Susie mean?" we asked.

"Susan is a lily flower. It's an old Hebrew name. Let's all write S-u-s-a-n." And that's what we did.

When Mama said, "Set the table, Sister," that was our signal to go do other interesting things.

Susie was in charge of the dishes. She set the table just the way Mama taught her. After the meal she washed and dried the china. Then she very carefully returned each piece to its assigned place on the shelves built along the wall.

I mostly avoided social encounters unless my brother was there to speak for me. But Jonas Long and his wife Midge came to be part of our household, and I felt brave with them. Midge worked inside, and I loved the way she made the window glass sparkle. She showed me how to bring a polish to the woodwork, and that was a job I was proud to do.

Gradually I began to spend some time in the garden with Jonas, pulling weeds and bringing water from the well. "Now, this here is the place where the tomato comes," he told me, pointing his brown finger carefully to a tiny yellow flower. "Mind you don't break off any flowers when you put the water there." He showed me just the right way to water the plants. "The flower is the mother, and the fruit is her child," he explained. Jonas inspired me with his wisdom, which he delivered with tenderness.

John spent his time out in the barn. My brother loved going out there, but I avoided it. The barn smelled of mold. The doors creaked, and a low moaning breeze haunted the place. In my mind it held dark mystery and felt spirit-possessed. Tools from the previous owners were left behind out there, and that was part of the intrigue for a curious boy like John. He spent hours rummaging through the stacks of forgotten carpenter things or carving on a bit of wood.

"Hey, Nosey Rosie, what did you find today?" I would tease him.

In one corner of the barn was a stack of supple cow hides, cured by someone from the past. Daddy cut the hides into manageable sizes and restacked them. He cleaned and sorted the tools, and generally made himself a workshop out there.

"Syd, come out here with me," my brother coaxed me from the garden one day. He was quiet and secretive.

"What are you up to now?" I asked.

He crouched low, as if sneaking. He curled his hand to bid me follow him and led me into the barn. In the corner where Daddy had taken away the cow hides, John discovered an empty corn crib. The structure had walls of open rails that sat close together at the floor and slanted out toward the top where they were attached to a wide rail. Now it was covered with sections of tree limbs all trimmed and waiting to be split for the fire.

John crawled between the limbs and peeked out through the slats. "This can be our secret hiding place." he said in an excited whisper. "How do you spell private?"

I only knew it started with P. "Stay right here, and I'll go check." I ran to the house and got the spelling book. Then I rushed back out to join him in the barn.

"Look in section two with the regular words," he said.

"Price . . . prim . . . pri . . . pri . . . private. P-r-i-v-a-t-e."

He took a sharp knife and carved his claim along the wooden railing.

And so it was his special place. He hid potentially useful bits of rope, interesting stones, and other such treasures there. When John went missing, I could usually find him out there.

They called me Sydna, sometimes Syd, short for Sydnie. According to *The Bryer New American Spelling Book*, my name literally means wide river valleys. It originated with St. Denys, who carried his head in his own hands to his own grave in France. My name was darkly prophetic, in spite of all the love that came when they called me. My family didn't know that in time I would walk wide river valleys, with my head in my hands, approaching my own early grave.

Fall 1823 – Jonas and Midge Long

"It's been a lovely day," Daddy said to Mama as they sat in the rocking chairs by the fire.

Since the arrival of Mr. Joshua Morgan, Mama kept her Bible on the little table between the rocking chairs. It became our family practice to gather there in the evenings. Mama read her Bible and shared her thoughts with us. One chilly fall night while I was embroidering flowers on a sampler, and John was on the floor next to me playing with a top, I stopped my stitching to listen.

"Yes, George. It has been a very nice day. But, you know, I couldn't do all this without Jonas and Midge." It was the first time I heard Mama even hint of being stressed. "I look forward every morning to those two walking through that door."

I knew she was right. Midge kept the windows spotless, polished the floors, and made sure Mama's hams were ready to serve at one o'clock. Jonas grew the vegetables, greeted the carriages, and kept the outside of the place looking just perfect. A hug from Midge or a wink from Jonas was as natural as anything else that happened in our home. To my mind they were family. Hearing what Mama said sparked an idea in my brain.

Daddy reached over, squeezed Mama's hand, and went back to reading his weekly *Liberty-Hall Gazette*.

The next morning I waited for Daddy in the porch swing. He came out and sat next to me to pull on his boots. I approached him with my idea.

"Daddy, I wanted to ask you … I mean … I think … could it be that Jonas and Midge might just stay here with us?"

He shot a look down at me. I knew I had said something wrong, but I didn't know what. I tried to explain. "I mean if Mama said it was okay, they wouldn't have to walk from town every morning." My daddy seemed to be holding his breath, and I thought for a moment maybe I still didn't say it right. "They help us, and it just seems …." I could tell this idea wasn't going over well. Maybe he felt ill. Maybe my timing was wrong.

"No," he said more emphatically than he had ever said no before. "No, they are working people, just like anybody else. They have their own place in town." He looked at me as if there was more to say, but if there was, he never said it. He composed himself and with a softer voice said, "Now go get to your chores, and let's not have any more of this talk."

I was puzzled by his reaction to my idea, but I knew never to ask about that again. Daddy never really scolded us, especially for trying to be kind. I knew Jonas and Midge were special to him. In time I would come to understand the compassion that was hidden in his sharp reply.

Spring 1825 – Riding the Horses; John Gets his Red Cap

While the porch swings and the barn made our lives at the inn pleasant enough, I thought the best thing about our inn was its location. It was within walking distance of Uncle Thomas's farm where the race horses lived. Susie cared nothing for being out-doors, but my brother and I thrived outside.

Our favorite days started just as the sun appeared. We begged off lessons, grabbed a chunk of bread for our breakfast and ran barefoot to the stables to meet our ten-year-old cousin, Jeb. By the time we reached him, mud was caked between our toes, but we didn't care. First, we watched the stable hands fill the troughs with golden grain. Then we'd grab a brush and rub those beautiful beasts, never mind we couldn't see past their bellies. We mostly saw them from underneath, looking past velvet noses into soulful eyes.

Finally our Uncle Thomas arrived and asked the question we lived to answer, "Are you ready to ride?"

"Me first, me first," we begged. I shook my hands and snapped my fingers in anticipation.

The trainers lifted us upon the backs of the colts. We held onto a smooth leather strap. The ka-thump, ka-thump of our rumps against their broad backs provided just the right weight for saddle-broke colts on practice runs around a small track, leaving a thin trail of dust behind us. Our little thighs ached as they held tight. The horsehair prickled our tender bare legs. But there was no place we'd rather be.

On my brother's sixth birthday, Uncle Thomas pulled a red bundle out of his pocket. "Little John, I have something for you." Our uncle plopped a wool cap on John's head. "See if you can make that fit," he laughed.

The cap was way too big for John, but he didn't care. He pulled it onto his head and let his ears stick out, flashing his toothy grin. Such was the cheerful character of our days on the farm, being loved and knowing we belonged. It was where I felt a seed of confidence.

Our days were long and lively then, but there were not enough hours in a day to exhaust our ambitions, our curiosities, and the goodness of our lives. We learned grace from our mother's hospitality. The beauty of nature's wonders came to us from our uncle's farm. Our doting Daddy D. cared for us with the love of any natural father. All I ever wanted or needed was to continue this joy of family and the simple celebration of human love that we knew at the Green River Inn.

If I could have seen down the road a ways, I might have stayed right there. Suffering was an idea from some other place. It only happened to other people. I didn't know the feeling—not yet.

January 1826 – John Finds a Leather Casing

My parents had the magnetic attraction of opposite poles. Mama's Warfield blood trickled all the way back to twelfth-century England. Warfield has nothing to do with war. No, it's a gentle name. It means a field of birds. Mama's name originated with people wanting a stable, loving family. That was Mama, and I took after her in that way.

Daddy Davis came from a long line of successful seafaring men who brought their shipping tradition from Wales to the port of Nantucket, Massachusetts. In contrast to Mama's domestic streak, Daddy's engine ran on adventure.

He loved telling us about the days of his own youth. "By the time I was Susie's age I was running a whole shoe factory by myself—trained all the apprentices and shipped the shoes on the Delaware River," he said. "I wanted to study law, but my father saw it differently; medicine, that was his idea. He wanted me to be a doctor. But I just couldn't abide spending my time with sick people. I went to the medical school to please him. But after a while, I just had to get away. That's when I found your mother in Cincinnati. That's how we all became a family." He retold us the story many times.

One day he came from the barn with a new shoe, freshly made with his own hands. A beautiful half-boot, it was. "I've still got it," he announced to us all. He pranced around the big table holding the boot above his head. He merrily returned to his barn. Within six months, he had hired three black men from Greensburg to apprentice, and soon they were all making shoes. Before long they had a whole cart of shoes. Daddy contracted with a trader who took the shoes to Cincinnati. When the man came back, he had a lot of nice things Mama wanted. She got thick rugs, cozy comforters, embroidered linens, some French hand cream, and her favorite thing—sweet-smelling soap to set by every wash basin.

And so it was that by the time I was nine years old our family had a routine, and life at Green River Inn had its rhythm. We three children had our part in the family, but life offered us opportunities to develop as individuals. Susie took great pride in her ability to keep the details of Mama's guests in her book. She put out the dishes and made sure the table was set exactly right. I learned gardening from Jonas, and Midge taught me how to bring a shine to the window glass. Seven-year-old John cherished his time out in the barn and made sure there was plenty of kindling for the fire.

"Syd, come see what I found." Little John fetched me from the garden and coaxed me to his special hiding place. In the late morning the sun shone bright outside, but the light dimmed inside the eerie barn. The big leaning door squeaked as we broadened the opening and walked through it. We stopped at the railing of the corn crib. I listened for the sound of the low moaning breeze while John disappeared under the timber wood. Then his face reappeared between the slats.

"You gotta come in here," he insisted.

I tucked my skirt between my knees and climbed in. The space was tight as we both huddled on our knees in the semi-darkness of the enclosure.

"Look!" He presented a banana-size sheath of fine leather.

"Where did you find this?" I took it in my hands.

"In the woods, while I was gatherin' kindlin'," he said. "Isn't it somethin'?"

It was impressive. A thin pocket of stiff leather, weathered over time, but still in very good condition. Brown leather was stitched with black leather lacing that made Xs on the long sides and across the bottom. A whip stitch finished off the opening edges. The initials JDS were stained in black on the front. A thin piece of leather hung off the back—a broken loop. Someone lost the sheath when it fell from his belt.

"Wow, that is something," I agreed.

"What do you think I should do with it?"

"Well, should we show it to Daddy?"

"That's what I thought." He looked a little sad at the idea of revealing his secret. John shoved the sheath into his pocket, and we crawled out of the corn crib. Reluctantly we walked to the inn and sat on the Saturday swing.

Daddy and Jonas came around the house with their arms full of carrots and cabbages. "Are you children about ready to eat?" Daddy smiled at us. I dodged the question and ducked my head, looking at my brother. Daddy gave Jonas his load of carrots and told him to go on in. Daddy came over to the swing. He pulled a big handkerchief from his pocket and wiped the back of his neck. "What are you up to now?" he asked, looking a little stern.

Hesitantly, John shimmied down and dug the sheath out of his pocket. He held it up to Daddy and confessed, "I found this."

Daddy's expression softened. "Well, I'll say. What is that?" He took it in his hands. "That's a mighty fine casing, son. Where did you find it?"

"In the woods while I was gettin' up kindlin'." John's face gleamed with confidence and hope.

After a brief inspection, Daddy handed it back. "Well, I don't know who it belongs to, or how it got in our woods, but I guess you can keep it till somebody else claims it."

John looked up at Daddy and grinned gratefully. He looked at me with relief and satisfaction as he pushed the stiff leather back down into his pocket. It was a moment of affirmation to have our Daddy's alliance. Daddy opened the great door, and we all went in to have our dinner.

June 1826 – December 1828 – Daddy's Lawyer Friend

Our home sat on the main road to Greensburg, the county seat of Green County, Kentucky. Greensburg was full of folks wanting work, and our inn was near enough for day workers to come and go. It was most convenient. In fact it was unavoidable to travelers going in and out of Greensburg. Lots of folks went to the county courthouse every day. In the summer of 1826, a dandy lawyer paid a visit to our inn. This particular solicitor found it necessary to pass our way regularly. He became our daddy's friend.

"My stay with your family is the only pleasant part of my journey," he said. Mr. Jeffery Schmidt had business that took him from the Tennessee state line up through Greensburg and Lexington and on to Washington, D.C. On the occasion of his visits, Daddy made a place for Mr. Schmidt to sit near him in the dining room for a meal or in the parlor chairs for a conversation.

"I heard speeches by Mr. Henry Clay when I lived in Philadelphia," my daddy said. Having a lawyer friend fulfilled a longing in Daddy's life. He had a hunger to talk about politics, government, and law.

"Now, there is a fine man, George." Mr. Schmidt took a slow draw of his cigar.

The two of them sat many nights by the light of our oil lamp. They discussed things I couldn't keep track of, the words got so particular. Solicitor Schmidt shared his law books and papers with Daddy. A pile of reading material soon claimed a corner of the space behind the stairway.

Midge joked about it when she polished the floor in there. "That lawyer man might just move in here and have himself an office this much closer to the courthouse, Mr. George," she teased. When I dusted the rocking chairs, I noticed how big the pile was growing.

I couldn't understand the bulk of what they said, but I recognized that Daddy and Mr. Schmidt shared soulful ideas. They didn't intend for me to be a party to their conversations, but I found a way to eavesdrop. It became necessary to dust the parlor furniture when Mr. Schmidt was in. I took my time to give an extra polish to the stair railings when they were in the parlor. They discussed geography, politics, and the government of the United States. They also discussed bondage and freedom.

"Slavery is a blight on humanity," Daddy said. "It goes against nature, and it goes against God."

"Yes, George, and we must find a way to put an end to the practice in this country."

Their voices would go soft and low, and I would have to leave before I understood it all. But I finally understood why Midge and Jonas couldn't live with us at the inn. Mr. Schmidt and my daddy agreed that all men should live free. Walking to work in the morning, and then walking back home at night was a sign of their independence. I felt a little ashamed for wanting them for ourselves. The men who made the shoes in our barn were contract labor. They were free to come and go, to work or not work. I was beginning to understand those things.

In 1828, Mr. Schmidt brought Daddy some thought-provoking papers with a powerful claim. Mr. Schmidt said that men from the United States were contracting to take families into Mexico. A Mr. Austin and a Mr. DeWitt, both politicians from the Missouri Territory, sent paper advertisements to Mr. Schmidt hoping he would spread them around. The inn was a perfect place for the advertisements. The day the papers came to the inn, Daddy didn't go to the barn at all. He sat on the front porch and discussed the situation.

"They ran Spain out back in '21. Now Mexico is colonizing the northern territories. The Mexican government is styled just like here, but they won't have bondage. Their laws don't allow it. They grant land by the thousands of acres to folks settling there. You can get it for twelve cents an acre," Mr. Schmidt explained.

"Thousands of acres?" Daddy asked the question again to be sure he understood it right. "How does that work, Schmidt?"

"You can buy your own claim outright, or you can partner with somebody to share the cost. No cash needed. You can pay over some years. You just have to pay thirty dollars to the Mexican government in the first six years you live there," Schmidt said.

My father was spellbound.

That evening Daddy sat on the edge of a big blue chair in the parlor, elbows on his legs. His hands were fisted and nervously punching into each other as he took in the details of the Mexican offer.

"How many miles from us is this settlement?" Daddy wanted to know. "What route are folks taking? What about these Indian raids we hear about down there? What is the best time of the year to make such a trip?" Daddy repeated his questions, and Mr.

Schmidt graciously repeated his answers. Daddy especially wanted to be sure about the land grants and the wildlife. From the day the papers arrived, our daddy was engrossed. His sense of adventure inflamed him, and he couldn't let go of the images in his head.

One night, Susie took Mr. Schmidt's papers and pinned them along the front of the big desk for everyone to see. On that night the promise of Mexico became my daddy's obsession.

January 1829 – June 1830 – Daddy's Obsession

George Washington Davis became a restless man. What he read in that pile of papers and what he saw on those advertisements disturbed him greatly. It disturbed him because he wasn't part of it. He came to believe Mexico was the new promised land. He imagined fields of native grasses just waiting to be grazed by the buffalo, and miles of black land dirt ready to be plowed into rows. He visualized rolling hills spilling into meadows of pecan trees needing to be harvested, and a network of rivers and creeks flowing over with fresh water, plump crawfish, and oysters. He imagined having thousands of acres with all these things for his very own.

Daddy imagined walking out his front door into a wilderness bustling with wildlife. He wanted to bring a deer home from a hunt and let the butchered animal cure a whole season in his own smokehouse. If anyone could claim a thousand acres, it should be George Davis.

In the evenings after our supper before he settled into his rocking chair to read, he stood in the parlor of the Green River Inn, puffing on his pipe. As the sun went down, he paced and paused at the window, hands in his pockets, looking longingly down the south road. He tapped the tobacco into place and relocated the mouthpiece of his pipe. He lifted his chin, squinting into the future. He was in a trance, considering his options.

After a while, he rubbed his chin, shook his head, and came back to us with a conversation about it. "Sydna, what would you think about us having our own farm? Wouldn't that be something?"

"Yes, Daddy, that would be fun. Could we have horses?"

"Yes, of course, some horses, and maybe some goats for milk and cheese. Maybe I'd cure my own leather. Goatskin is very soft. I bet I could make gloves. And cows—we'd need cowhides for boot leather."

John came in with his red wool cap, jumped on Daddy's lap, and agreed. "Yes, Daddy, horses, our very own horses."

Daddy persuaded us with what he knew would appeal to each of his children and Mama. None of it appealed to Susie. Mama listened. Each evening we all gathered in the parlor to hear our daddy's thoughts.

Mr. Schmidt arrived one early morning after Mama and Susie took the carriage into Greensburg. Mr. Schmidt didn't stay overnight that time. He stopped just long enough to talk to Daddy. They talked just inside the front door where I was polishing the window glass.

"Good morning, George. I got home last month and realized I've lost my best knife. Did you find it around here?"

"I'll have to ask Susie when she gets back from Greensburg," Daddy said. That seemed to satisfy Mr. Schmidt, and he went on his way.

When Susie and Mama returned, Daddy asked about the knife. "Yes, it's here," Susie said.

She leaned into the vault and brought out a small brown bundle with Schmidt written on the outside. She unwrapped the paper and handed a knife to Daddy. His eyes widened as he inspected it, and he got a puzzled look on his face. "Where is your brother?" he asked me.

"I'll go find him," I said. John was in the woods with his little cart, collecting kindling. I found him lying on the ground, legs crossed, looking up into the sky. "You need to come to the house," I told him. "Daddy wants you."

He sat up, hooked his ankles, and linked his arms around his knees, his head cocked to one side. "What for?"

"I don't know. I think he wants to ask you something."

I helped him turn the cart, and we headed in the direction of the inn.

Daddy met us on the path. He pointed a hand in the direction of the barn. "You got that sheath out there in your hideaway?"

"Yes, Daddy. Why?" John asked, shielding his eyes from the sun.

"Look at this, son." He opened his hand to reveal a long slender knife. The handle was wrapped with black lacing.

John gently removed the knife from Daddy's hand. "Oh, look," he said as he let a lot of air out of his lungs. "Is that the same black lacing that's on the sheath I found?"

"Well, we need to see about that."

John stood for a moment, turning the knife in his hands. Slowly he nodded his head. Then he gave Daddy the knife, and we all walked into the barn. Once inside, John slipped into the crib and in a short time was out again with the sheath. He handed it to Daddy. We all three stood with our heads bowed together comparing the black leather Xs on the sheath and the covering of the handle of the knife. They were the same.

Daddy took the sheath. "JDS," he said as he ran his thumb over the black initials. "Jeffrey something Schmidt; it has to be his."

John and I looked at each other, surprised at the connection to Daddy's friend.

"But how did it get in our woods?" John wondered out loud.

"I don't know, but we'll find out. I'll ask him tomorrow night when he comes back through here. What do you think we should do if the knife is his?"

John took only a second to answer. "If the knife is his, we need to give it back," he said. "He might need it."

Daddy smiled a proud smile. "That's right, son. But I still want to know how it got into our woods. So, I'll tell him I still have some questions about Mexico. He'll sit down with us, and then we'll ask him about this knife."

Mr. Schmidt didn't return when we expected. We were aching with curiosity, waiting and wondering when he would come back and what he would say.

What if he is a bad man? Or maybe he's been watching us from the woods, I thought as we waited through the hours, hoping Mr. Schmidt had a plausible explanation.

It was several days later in the afternoon when Mr. Schmidt finally returned. He signed in the book at the desk with Susie. "Did you find my knife, young lady?"

"I think so, sir. You'll have to ask Daddy about it."

Later at the supper table, Daddy told Mr. Schmidt he had more questions about the immigration program, and our guest agreed heartily to another discussion in the parlor. "Sure, Davis. And by the way, did you find that knife of mine?"

"We might have. We need to take a look at that."

John poked me with his elbow, and he went straight away to find a place to sit on the floor next to the rocking chairs. He thumbed through the papers on Daddy's reading pile and pretended to be interested in them. Mama coaxed him to come eat, but his appetite was satisfied in record time that night. Finally Daddy and Mr. Schmidt sat on the blue chairs. John and I huddled on the floor half a room away.

"Schmidt, I think I have some good news for you," Daddy said.

Then he pulled out the knife and handed it to his friend. Mr. Schmidt smiled and thanked Daddy.

"But I have to be straight with you," Daddy continued. Mr. Schmidt looked puzzled. Daddy pulled out the sheath. "What can you tell me about this?" Daddy held out the leather pocket with the initials.

Mr. Schmidt went stiff and his eyes went wide. He winced a bit, took in some air, and blew it out of his mouth. He cocked his head to one side and nodded. "Yes, that was mine, too."

"But how did it get into our woods?" Daddy asked, shaking the sheath towards his friend.

Mr. Schmidt sighed deeply, pushed back, and rested his head against the back of the big blue chair. "It's because of my brothers," he said quietly.

"What?"

"Davis, I'll tell you," Mr. Schmidt began. "This inn has been one of my favorite places for two reasons. In recent years I enjoyed coming here because of your family. But long ago, because it was … it belonged to my family," he said.

John's mouth dropped open and his eyes bugged out. I ducked my head just a bit and shook it, reminding my brother to stay quiet.

Daddy put his head to one side and settled into his chair to listen. They were quiet. "Go on."

"I have two brothers. Edgar, the oldest, is an artist. He did all the detail work in this place." Schmidt waved his hand toward the ornate stair railings. "The man can do anything with his hands. People all over the county hired him and paid him well."

I studied the carved wood on the risers of the steps. I recalled that even our home in Cincinnati didn't have such detail.

Mr. Schmidt went on. "Edgar bought this inn to give our youngest brother a job. But our brother Carter was no-account. He was a drinker, a fighter, and a dealer." Mr. Schmidt looked down at the floor and shook his head.

I felt embarrassed for him.

"Edgar Schmidt is a respected name around these parts, all the way to Tennessee. He built that barn so he could cure hides and work his wood. The old hides you found out there were his."

My brother flashed me a look of concern.

"He made this knife and scabbard for me. My middle name is David, JDS." He pointed to each letter. "Edgar spent his time curing leather and making beautiful things. Our little brother was just as talented, but he only made trouble." Mr. Schmidt leaned forward and put an elbow on each knee.

John linked his arms around his crossed knees and strained his neck toward the leather piece in Mr. Schmidt's hand.

"Carter Schmidt was a big man, but he had an affliction that made him feel small and simple. He was the only one of us to keep up the German language our grandparents spoke. He spoke with a German accent. And he was something called tongue-tied."

John jolted a bit at the thought of it.

"He sounded funny when he talked. People asked him to repeat himself. Sometimes they laughed. No one meant any harm. It was just funny. But Carter couldn't see the humor. He was always, always getting in a fight."

I thought about Mr. Schmidt's description. I rubbed my tongue against the top of my mouth and wondered how it could ever be tied.

"Edgar and I told Carter he had to get control of himself. But he didn't. He just sat on the porch out there and waited for opportunities to come find him. He made deals he couldn't keep, but he didn't care. He made a deal for a horse on that farm next over, just past Thomas."

I remembered the beautiful woods on the other side of our uncle's farm, and the animals that lived there.

"The fact that he couldn't pay for the horse didn't matter to him. He brought the horse here for one night, and the next morning Carter and the horse were gone."

I looked at my brother. He was lost in the story of the criminal brother. He didn't associate crime with Mr. Schmidt.

"The man who was owed for the horse came looking for Carter. He found me inside. I told him Carter was gone, but he didn't believe me. He went out to the barn in a rage and attacked Edgar. I followed him out there, and the three of us rolled around together. I pulled my knife. I never intended to use it, and I threw it down at some point. I guess the loop of my scabbard broke, and it fell off me."

Mr. Schmidt looked at John. We were all quiet for a short time. I was sorting out the images of three grown men brawling in our barn.

"After it was all over, I found the knife, but I never did find the scabbard. It probably got dragged out of the barn by some varmint in the quiet years around here before you folks bought the inn. I'd really like to have it all back," Mr. Schmidt concluded

"Where are your brothers now?" Daddy asked as he handed the scabbard to Mr. Schmidt.

"Edgar went to New Orleans, and Carter disappeared. I never heard from him since. I don't know if I'll ever know where he is. I see Edgar when I can. I just keep on with my own business and try to do good by my own name. I thank you for recovering this and for letting me explain." He pointed the leather pocket towards Daddy and then held it to his chest.

Daddy nodded his head in acknowledgment of the gratitude. He looked down at his own boots for a time. "So it was your older brother Edgar who left all those tools out there?" Daddy asked.

"Yep. He left it all. He just wanted to start over fresh. He's a gentle soul, and he just wanted to put all this behind him."

Daddy shook his head. I sat there on the floor, imagining how it would be to have my little brother missing from my life and to have Susie trying to defend our good family name. John looked at me with big eyes. He tightened the muscles in his lips making his expression of sympathy.

"I'm glad to know the truth," Daddy said, reaching out his hand. Mr. Schmidt leaned forward and sat up a little straighter as the two men shook hands. "And we have my son to thank for finding your scabbard." Daddy looked around for John.

My brother got up and sheepishly walked over there. Daddy slicked back John's cowlick. "John wanted to find the rightful owner, didn't you, son?" John nodded his head.

Mr. Schmidt shook John's hand in a kindly way. "I sure thank you."

"Now tell me the worst of what might await us if I were to take up this notion of going to Mexico."

Daddy put an arm around my brother's waist and John stood with his hands on Daddy's leg, waiting to hear what Mr. Schmidt would say.

Mr. Schmidt leaned forward and slid the long knife into its scabbard. Without words, he placed the recovered pieces into the shaft of his boot. Then he sat back and cupped one fisted hand into the other. He crossed his foot on his knee, tilted his head, and squinted his left eye till it almost closed.

"Davis, I really don't know. We can only know what people are saying. Mexico needs settlers. If a man can get there, he can claim his own headright. The head of a family has a right to buy over 4,000 acres of land, and you can get it cheap. Why, even barons in England don't claim that big a spread." He laughed, slapped his leg, and measured out a wide space with his arms. The two men waited while the images seeped in.

Then quietly, as if not wanting anybody else to hear, he leaned in and almost whispered, "A man can live off his land, Davis. All you need is maybe a vegetable garden with a few chickens." His hands motioned to the floor. "They produce a few eggs for you, and maybe you trade some. A man might consider cattle or goats for milk and meat."

"Then I could cure the leather." Daddy glanced up to the ceiling and leaned back with his fingers linked behind his head. John sat down beside me on the floor.

"They say wild turkeys are just waiting outside a man's cabin door, practically offering themselves for a family feast." Mr. Schmidt spoke with a tight jaw, quietly letting his words out sparingly. "You'll have rivers and creeks for fresh water, and they're just crawling with prawns." He shook his head as if even he found it hard to believe. "I'd go myself, but I'm already committed to my clients for years to come. Here, let me show you a letter I got recently." Mr. Schmidt took a folded paper from his coat pocket.

Daddy read it aloud.

To whom it may concern:

We are the Cunninghams from Virginia, come to DeWitt Colony.

It is a good land with abundant wildlife and fresh water. The land is an expanse of green grazing with stands of cedar elms along the Guadalupe River. Tracts at high elevation may be obtained from Mr. DeWitt, and he will assure the claims. One makes a peaceful home with romantic scenery. The air is so pure that during the summer evenings we find pleasure to sleep in the open spaces under a sky of splendorous stars. We hold the hope of our better future with increased population.

Help of any kind needed is available among the neighbors of our community.

Mr. Schmidt went on. "You only need three things to qualify for land in Mexico." He held out three fingers and pointed to each finger as he listed the three requirements. "First, a person must pledge to be Christian, and vow loyalty to the Catholic Church. Second, you must have a skill to help support your community. And third, you need to bring letters of testimony, stating your good moral character." Mr. Schmidt searched my father's face. Quietly he said, "George, I think you would do well in Mexico."

"Can you take a letter from me to this Mr. DeWitt and see what he says?"

"Sure, Davis. That's a good idea."

"I'll just ask what kind of offer he can make us, and then we'll see what we should do."

The next morning Mr. Schmidt and Daddy drank coffee on the Saturday swing. "I don't know how long it will take to get an answer, Davis. But I'll do all I can to find out more information for you."

I felt comforted in my heart as Mr. Schmidt rode away with Daddy's letter in his bags.

June 1830 – November 1830 – Mama Agrees to Go to Mexico

In the summer of 1830, we were all sitting in the parlor one day and my mama brought up her concerns about immigrants going to Mexico. Daddy shared with her the details just as Mr. Schmidt had listed them. Mama listened, nodding her head as she took in each qualification. When he told her about the Catholic obligation, she stopped him. "George, we're Methodist."

In fact, we were more Methodist than we had ever been, with holding Sabbath in our home. Mr. Joshua Morgan delivered a piano to our inn, and he made even more frequent visits to help Susie learn to play the hymns on it. Mama was sure we would be Methodists forever.

"Won't matter," Daddy said. "When they ask us if we're loyal to the Catholic Church, we say yes, and that's not a lie. Would we disrupt the Catholics?" He looked around. "No, we would not. Would we be troublesome to the Catholics?" With a wave of his hand, he stood waiting for Mother's reply. "No," he said while she was still thinking about it. "We can learn some Catholic prayers and show our support," he concluded with one hand on his hip and the other holding the bent wood of a dining room chair.

In the following months when Mr. Schmidt stayed with us, we had more family meetings to discuss the possibilities with him. Daddy was ready to pack, but Mama had concerns.

"What shall we do if the children become ill?" She pleaded her case with a palm stretched out in my direction. "How will we protect ourselves from Indians?" She clenched her hands to her chest. "I … I don't …." She couldn't finish. Her concerns were so overwhelming she couldn't find the words for them. Mama looked at Daddy, not knowing what to say. She twisted a linen handkerchief between her hands.

"Now, Rebecca, we'll get all those things sorted out." He put a hand on each of her shoulders. "With all the folks down there already, you know they have their ways. Becka, you know, if it wasn't working out, they'd all be back."

Mama seemed more composed and sank down in one of the blue chairs, fanning herself with the handkerchief.

The alliance between Mr. Schmidt and my daddy tightened. "George, I'll write you a letter of introduction, and I'll mention all the talent this family brings. You know law. You have some schooling in medicine. You are good with your hands, and you're sociable folks." He counted on his fingers again as he listed our qualifications. "I dare say you could have your pick of the land and be frontrunners for that program down there."

Daddy re-lit his pipe. He glanced at Mama, who sat with her hand over her mouth just shaking her head. Susie sat cleaning her fingernails. John and I sat on the floor, taking it all in.

Another day Mr. Schmidt came with even more enthusiasm for the immigration program. He began to explain to Daddy that the rules about Mexico were not really being enforced. Word was that the social status of a migrant was irrelevant in Mexico. If the letters of testimony could be obtained, past sins were erased upon arrival. Obligations of debt and crime were dropped at the border like a pair of dirty trousers. If a man could make the trip, his history would begin again. Rumors bubbling up from the south suggested that Mexico was so anxious for settlers they avoided checking any papers or confirming church affiliation. He told our mama, "Miss Rebecca, I don't think anyone will care if you are Methodist."

Mr. Schmidt went on. "George, there's men going down there just to keep out of jail. They just leave word that they've gone to Mexico, and the law doesn't bother with them anymore."

Mama gasped and flashed a look at Daddy as her eyes grew bigger.

"DeWitt would be proud to have a man like you in his outfit," Mr. Schmidt said.

Daddy looked at Mama and moved his pipe to the other side of his mouth. "Let's just see what comes of all this. No sense getting upset over what we don't even really know."

During the next year Mr. Schmidt returned to us empty-handed several times. But finally, in the late summer of 1830 he appeared at our door with a smile and some good news.

"I got a letter for you, George." He handed Daddy a folded paper.

Daddy took the paper and opened it. As his eyes followed the lines of script, a smile spread across his face.

Daddy was welcome to bring us all to Mexico. "No place on earth can exceed this for beauty," the letter said. "You will not be disappointed."

Cheap land, forgiven debts, a fresh start—it was tempting for a lot of Americans. And it was an irresistible challenge for the upstanding citizen, George Washington Davis.

Ambitious folks have a way of coaxing the glamour out of a thing, and they avoid any notions that work against their case. I couldn't imagine how life could be any better than the one we had in Kentucky. But I was young. I adopted my father's dream. We all did, even Mama. On the basis that others had gone and seemed happy, she agreed to go.

They told us on a brisk fall Sunday at the 1:00 dinner table, after the ham and before the apple pie. We would be leaving in the winter. Christmas of 1830 would be our last season in the United States.

Later, when I looked back, I wondered how we could have been so naive. How could we not realize the convenience of a well already dug, with a pump bringing water right into the kitchen? How could we overlook the comfort of sitting on the fine furniture we had in the inn? We didn't consider the luxury of a road already bricked and the security of looking through windows of real glass. If we had sat in the late night around Daddy's rocking chair and considered the dark possibilities of losing all our comforts, we might have stayed behind. But we never had that conversation. Mama may have thought it, but she loved Daddy Davis and trusted his vision.

During life on earth, especially for the young, folks don't really know what they have until it's gone. And so, not knowing, we bought into the adventure that would take us to Coahuila y Tejas.

December 1830 – Sydnie Decides to Go to Mexico

Determination outweighed limited means, and Daddy was determined. There were no riverboats running when Daddy wanted to leave Kentucky, so he negotiated a deal with a merchant running a flatboat hauling flour out of Kentucky to New Orleans the first week in January 1831. We would travel with the flour, and Daddy would work for our passage. He was pleased with himself for getting the family fare for free, and he'd pocket a bit of extra money to help finance the move.

I'm not sure when or if Daddy slept during the month of December. He was consumed with sorting and packing for our big adventure. He was especially committed to returning at least some of the tools Mr. Edgar Schmidt left in the barn.

"If Edgar is in New Orleans, we can find him. Those knives won't be any trouble, and it's a small thing we can do." He put a wooden tool chest under the steps of the front porch.

Susie was twenty-one and in love with the Reverend Joshua Morgan. She decided to stay in Kentucky. I was thirteen and my brother John was eleven. It's a natural thing for children to grow up and make their own lives, but I wasn't quite ready to disassemble my family. I cried many a December night, wondering how long till I'd see my sister again and knowing for sure I'd never again see Midge and Jonas. Mama heard me crying and came into the room.

"What's wrong, Sydnie?" She pulled a little stool up next to my bed.

I turned over, and she took my hand in hers. "I want to be with you and Daddy, and with John, but I'll miss Susie and the inn, and our life here, Mama. I know I should be happy about going, but I can't feel the happiness."

The moonlight came into the room through the window, illuminating her face. Her loving eyes drew the confusion right out of me. I could feel myself letting go of it. "I understand. You go to sleep now, and we'll sort it out tomorrow." She placed a hand on each of my shoulders as she bent over to leave a kiss on my wet cheek. I turned back onto my side and Mama tucked the muslin coverlet around me. Her comforting ways gave me peace for the rest of the night.

I didn't waste any time the next day. "Good morning, Mama. When can we talk about going to Mexico?" I dipped a clean face cloth in the big water basin Jonas filled every morning and rubbed it against my eyelids.

"I spoke to George last night." Mama took the cloth and wiped my entire face. "You were so upset, and I want you to feel certain about this. Give him a day or two, and we'll see what he can work out."

"Yes, Mama." I really was relieved. I knew they would find a way to help me decide.

A few days later our parents called us in to sit at the big table for a serious conversation. Daddy did all the talking. "Your Uncle Thomas has agreed to take you in if you don't want to go with us to Mexico," he said. "You think about it. We love you, and we'll support you with whatever you decide." I looked at my brother who was sitting with his head propped on a dirty fist.

Jonas and Midge stood in the doorway. Daddy turned to them. "Thomas needs good help on his place. He would like you both to come work with him if that suits you. But if you want to do something else, you let me know. I'll do whatever I can to leave you well fixed."

Later that evening I sought out my mother's counsel. "Mama, what should I do?" I asked in bewilderment. "I still can't decide. I love Uncle Thomas and the horses, but it won't be the same with you gone, and the inn won't be our home."

"Life is full of choices, child." She finished the dishes in the basin and dried her hands on her apron. "Sometimes there is more than one right answer. You just say your prayers and ask for a sign," she said as she walked into the front parlor. "I can't make the decision for you." She sat down in one of the big blue chairs, and I sat in the other.

Mama took my hands and spoke gently to me. "Sydna, close your eyes." I did. "Now, imagine you're grown, like Susie is now." I did; it made me smile. "Now, where are you? Are you in a big field, maybe with some horses of your own? Do you see a big, wide sky? Who is with you?"

I opened my eyes.

"No, you keep those peepers closed, young lady." She laughed and touched my nose. I laughed and closed my eyes again. "Can you see where you are? Think about that until I count to five."

By the time she counted to five, I had been to Mexico and back to Kentucky several times.

". . . Four, five."

I opened my eyes and looked at my mother.

"Sydna, hindsight seems so much clearer than looking ahead into the unknown. Maybe you can imagine doing something; then look back at it, as if it already happened. Then you can see how you feel. See if you feel regretful or if you feel glad about what you chose. That's all I know to do."

"Thank you, Mama." I gave her a hug and she went back to the kitchen. I still didn't know what I should do. *She's treating me like an adult*, I thought. *Like she treated Susie when we first came here.* As a budding teenager, I was realizing true changes in my body, in my mind, and in the way my parents talked to me.

I thought about independence and facing adult choices. I tried to imagine myself in Mexico. Then I imagined myself in Kentucky. I kept a simple prayer on my mind. *Show me your sign, Lord,* I repeated over and over again.

It was my job to beat the rugs as everyone was getting ready for Christmas. Jonas and John took the rugs out and hung them on low limbs of the oak tree by the barn. I went to the barn and got a rug beater the Schmidt brothers left out there. It was a heavy wire beater with a good handle I could grip. I walked through the shallow crust of ice left by the last snowfall, crunching my way to the tree with the rugs.

Along the way I saw something bright red in contrast with the blanket of white covering the ground. John's cap had fallen off, and he left it there in his icy tracks. I picked it up. In a moment of time I imagined myself in the future, without my brother. If my brother was gone, and if that cap was all we had to remember him, would I want to give up the years we could still have together?

I tucked the cap in the tree where the branches came together. I stood there for a time, looking at the cap. Maybe that's what John would decide. Maybe this was my sign, to go or stay as my brother chose.

I hit the first rug. Dust flew from the heavy mat. A strange satisfaction overtook me. I hit it again, and the sensation returned. The rays of the sun on that December day warmed the chill in the air. My exertion generated warmth from deep inside, while the cold air chilled my cheeks and my forehead, damp with perspiration. To go or stay was the question burning in my soul. I was comforted only by the assurance that I'd have the love of family either way.

I beat those rugs until my arms ached and I was breathing heavily. Then I took the cap and went to find my brother. He was in the woods dumping the ash from the fireplace.

"Here's your cap," I said.

He took it from me, slapped it against his knee and plopped it on his head.

"What do you think, John? Are you going to Mexico?" I asked.

"Of course," he said with a smile. "Come on, Syd. You gotta come with us."

That was my sign. I was loved, and I was wanted. I would go to Mexico with my brother.

So on the coldest day of the year, we packed our clothes in canvas bags. Joshua Morgan came to see us off. Susie hugged Mama, and through their tears, they promised to send a letter by way of Mr. Schmidt. Daddy took the wooden toolbox from under the steps and loaded it along with all our other important things onto a stagecoach out of Greensburg. We took the north road to Louisville and made our way to the docks. Daddy found the man who agreed to take us on his barge, and our journey began.

January 2, 1831 – Leaving Louisville; Down the Ohio River; On to the Mississippi River

My brother reveled in the excitement of the flatboat, driven by his natural curiosity and gusto. He was a boy on a boat, bursting with desire to be a man. John quickly knew every crew member by name, and he joined them in as much as they would tolerate from him. And tolerate they did, even encouraging him to pull rope and tote tools. Before the sun was up, John was grinning at my daddy, pulling at his sleeve, eager to start another day. With his face reddened by the wind, and with that cap pulled down so his ears stuck out, John ran (never walked) in his adventure on our cruise along the Ohio River and then into the flow of the mighty Mississippi River.

Aside from the inspiration it provided my brother, the river cruise made little impression on me. Mother and I took naps and observed the work. Like a queen and her lady-in-waiting, we wrapped ourselves in quilts, sat on the flour sacks, and watched the countryside pass by.

The Mississippi was a wide spread of water, but we could always see one bank. The brown of winter woods gave way to the checkerboard of rooftops as tiny towns fell in line. A ribbon of white curled along the bank where the water lapped against ports and docks. It was beautifully monotonous, as lovely as the silent paintings I once saw in a Greensburg art display.

In truth, Mother began a most unfortunate condition on that trip. Exposure to the damp and cold brought on an unprecedented bursitis. I first noticed that she hesitated to turn her head unless absolutely necessary, and then often with a grimace. Her neck was stiff, and her eyes betrayed the pain she wanted to keep private. Her stiff fingers were soon unable to grip the railing when she moved about. She became unstable in her efforts to get up from our benches. Much as she tried to conceal it, I took notice of her knees on the rare occasion they were exposed. She blamed her difficulties on the swaying of the boat. It didn't take long until I realized her trouble was red and swollen joints. But Mother would never complain, so I pretended not to know.

As we moved south, the scenery along the riverbank was our only entertainment. In the forested sectors between cities, the trees were still embraced in December snow. They held on to their icy lace as if just wanting to show off their beauty.

"Oh, Syd. Just look at those beautiful trees."

"Yes, Mother, they are lovely." I sighed.

I was truly bored with it all, but I tried to make it better than it really was. We had the good fortune to make brief stops in the cities of Memphis, Vicksburg, and other places along the way, but we stayed near the docks. After almost six weeks, when I wanted to scream with the boredom of it, a new excitement swept across the vessel. The captain shouted a new command, and the men ran to let out the ropes from where they were curled into giant circles. We felt our direction change, and I realized we were finally at the end of that part of our journey. The flatboat pulled into a slip alongside bigger boats. We had reached that place in Louisiana where the Mississippi spills into the Gulf of Mexico.

And so, the initial leg of our journey to Mexico was uneventful. It was our arrival in New Orleans that opened my eyes for the first time to a new culture.

February 8, 1831 – New Orleans

"Sydna, come take your brother's hand," my mother instructed me as we left the barge. Our legs wobbled with little control of our feet on the slimy surface of the gangway off the boat. Crowds of people pushed by us.

John took my hand, and I cautiously made my way forward. My eyes soon riveted on a man dressed in bright red and orange strips of fabric that flapped against his body as he walked. He was gyrating with a dance step in the direction from which I heard music. A ways down the street, more people were gathering in a market. They were dancing and waving their arms, chanting and making music as they paraded in small groups among the market sheds. My brother was fixated on the spectacle. His mouth dropped open. His feet walked south while his eyes faced north, fascinated with the brightly clothed man in the street. My senses weren't prepared for this barrage of sights and sounds. The place seemed awkwardly unrefined with loud music and people gyrating out in public. Our feet were slipping, and I was concerned with being thrown into the river.

This could be dangerous, I thought. I remembered Mama's stiffness and knew she couldn't protect us. I felt for the first time in my life the need to be brave. I took a deep breath, squared my shoulders, and looked at my brother.

"You hold my hand tight."

"Yes, Syd." My brother shot me a knowing glance. He knew I needed his courage more than he needed mine.

My mother's instructions to hold my brother's hand jolted my focus, and I realized I had to pay attention. I did just long enough to get us past the initial landing of the dock. We found a row of unattended crates where Mama could sit while Daddy got our bundles off the flatboat. I felt sheltered behind the crates. We settled ourselves a bit and took in the harbor pageantry.

Daddy and the boat hands put our things into a pile. It was a small mountain of canvas containing our past and a wooden box of tools. We each took a share, and Daddy loaded himself down like a packhorse. Mother walked with a limp. She had shuffled sometimes back in Kentucky, but rarely. She might have limped during the summer, in the late-night hours after she worked in the kitchen all day. But our trip down two rivers took a toll on her. Her face looked old, with great pools of blue-gray under her eyes. Her typical freshness was gone.

We trudged slowly, carrying all our baggage and wanting to see the curiosities of the strange place. We fell into the flow of other people coming from the harbor with their bundles. Along the boardwalk, we passed fishermen with barrels of their recent catch. They offered the fish for sale, waving the poor creatures in our faces as we passed. That pungent fish aroma just on the safe side of rotten landed heavily on the palate, way in the back of my mouth.

Further along we detoured our way around some ladies spilling out on the steps of a hotel. They reminded me of a flock of hens, laughing and clucking in a language I later learned was French. They were wrapped in gorgeous dresses—shiny ruby silk and rich green velvet hugging tiny waists, with crisp laces tucked in around their bosoms. *Rather scanty for the season,* I thought. I remembered Susie and wished she could see those ladies. *Could I wear a dress and look that pretty one day?* I dodged one lady who swung a tapestry bag gathered up by a slender leather leash. Her eyes were painted, and she looked beautiful and happy. I nodded politely to her, wanting to feel her happiness.

This place was a fascination of new mysteries. I stood for a moment, adjusting to the culture, and reminding myself that Daddy and Mama always knew how to make everything okay. But we still had far to go, and I still had much to learn.

We stopped in front of a narrow stoop. Three steps led to the narrow door of a pink brick structure marked HOTEL. "You children wait here with our bags until Mother and I can get a room." In a short time Daddy came back.

We each took some bags and went into the little hotel. John and I waited in the front room as Mama and Daddy collected our bundles. They made several trips to a room on the ground floor where we would stay until we could leave for Mexico. We stood there in the silence, observing the dark, small lobby of our temporary home. The only movement was a dog curled on the floor, licking his belly. An old woman sat like a statue at a narrow reception desk, reading a book. Two straight chairs stood in front of a narrow window. A tiny table sat between the chairs. It was very unlike the inn where we had slept just six weeks earlier. I felt a twinge of homesickness and wondered what Susie was doing.

Our parents took so long I went in search of them. I peeked into the first room of the short hall, and there they stood embraced in each other's arms. In spite of their exhaustion, they found the strength they needed to push on. Daddy seemed to have recovered, and fairly danced across the room.

"Let's go find some good food." Daddy took Mama's hand and helped her down the steps. I wondered if she finally admitted her discomfort. Daddy was very attentive to her.

The trickle of people in the street thinned, as folks found their destinations. Some waited for another boat. Others had come home. We fell into a path following the last of the travelers, looking for a café.

We turned off a side street and found ourselves caught up in a throng of people all looking to the center of a crowd. Daddy stopped and helped Mama settle on a bench built around a street lamp. Daddy looked around as if considering our next turn, maybe trying to decide the best direction to walk. Mama dropped her head to one side and rubbed her eyes. John sat beside her, snuggling in as close as he could get. He put his arm on Mama's knee and looked up into her face. Mama smiled at him and put her hand over his.

The tall people in front of me smelled of sweat. I went around behind my family to stand by Daddy. Then I looked at the crowd.

There in the center of all the people was a block of stone, just high enough for one step up. A very muscular black man stood alone on the stone. His eyes were closed, and his face was slightly lifted to the sky. His jaw was clenched, and his facial muscles rippled in the light of the late afternoon sun. He could have been an onyx statue and would not have been firmer and prouder. I realized he was the center of attention. There was a little gathering of dark folks standing nearby.

A white man was shouting at the crowd, pointing out the black man's physical assets. "This here is as fine a worker as you'll find. He's been the most productive cotton picker on the place, 'cordin' to Joseph Sprats, present owner."

Owner? The thought of it tightened in my gut. The man's eyes were closed, not because of the sun. It was because of the ignorance surrounding him. My innocent eyes recognized the grace in his shame. He was a paradox. While he appeared stronger than any man in the crowd, he stood at their mercy.

I remembered Midge and Jonas, and the shame I felt for wanting them to live with us. The man on the step could have been Jonas, and I knew Jonas was a man capable of many things. My eyes welled up with salty moisture. Gradually, after absorbing the unbelievable scene before us, I couldn't deny it. The man was being auctioned off like livestock.

A child clung to the long legs of a slender bronze woman. When the bidding ended, the noble black man turned to that woman, and they exchanged a look of sorrow that burned a little hole into my heart. I remembered my parents' embrace, and I knew that's what these two people wanted. I looked at my mother. Her mouth was agape, with her hand over it. Her eyes were wide with the brows pinched together, like those rare occasions when she scolded us. She looked at my daddy as she slid an arm around my brother and pulled him tightly to her.

John covered his face with his hands and refused to look up. I wiped my face with my sleeve and sniffed in the disgust that tried to drain from my nostrils. Daddy shook his head in subconscious disapproval. We all knew without saying; these were slaves, like the ones we'd heard defended in Ohio, and the ones we knew were working on farms in Kentucky. It was a slice of society in the United States that I knew was on my father's mind and that I had heard him discuss with Mr. Schmidt. Of all the good things Daddy told us about, seeing this never occurred to me. We signed on to do business in new places, and this was how business was done in New Orleans. It was my first glimpse of human indecency.

Daddy signaled us to go, and I was relieved when he led us into a little café around the corner. A man showed us to a table with four chairs. "We'll all have the bouillabaisse over bread," Daddy said. We sat in awkward silence, taking in the atmosphere of the tiny room full of mumbling voices and clanking glass. The soup was a novelty. Bits of fish, okra, and tomatoes captured in a thick, spicy broth, all soaked into a lump of soft dough with a crust. It was delicious, but I wondered what the black children were eating for their supper. We ate and returned to our hotel room for the night.

Daddy had business in New Orleans. He tucked the wooden toolbox under his arm and went to locate Mr. Edgar Schmidt. I wasn't there, but I saw the satisfaction on Daddy's face when he told us about it later. "It was a heartwarming thing to hand Edgar his box of knives. Those two could be twins," Daddy said about Edgar and Jeffery David. "That round face with those pudgy cheeks and buggy eyes; it was kind of amazing."

Daddy looked at Mama and cupped her hands inside of his. "Rebecca, I asked Edgar a special favor." Mama looked puzzled. "I asked him to be our courier. I've sent a letter to Susie to let her know we've come this far. He promised to help us get word when we get settled. We can send letters to him, and he'll pass them on to his brother. Jeffrey will take them back to Kentucky." Mother sank into Daddy's arms, closed her eyes, and smiled. For a brief moment we were all quiet, realizing the finality of our departure from the United States. Then, Daddy went to register us on a boat to cross the Gulf of Mexico. We stayed in New Orleans almost two weeks.

February 18, 1831 – Old Scotts on the Lavaca River

We left New Orleans with a thick, gray fog haunting the city. Moisture collected on my hair and cheeks as we walked to the harbor. Our family of four and about ten other passengers loaded onto a schooner called *Emblem*. She was rickety and loose. The weathered boards creaked as if complaining that we were walking upon them.

Panic set in as my feet touched the loading bridge. A growing dread left me almost unable to breathe, a tightness gripping my throat. I disguised my discomfort with a forced smile as we took our seats on benches, securing ourselves for the launching. I closed my eyes and heard the birds crying for fish, teased by the smell of those being sold near the docks. Anxiety grew and clenched my chest with a sharp pain.

A gale of wind broke through the fog. It drove our vessel as if to evict us from the city of New Orleans. Brisk February air mingled with the dampness and gave me a shiver. Then the magic of family affection rescued me. My brother wrapped my shoulders in his own wool jacket. Small as it was, it felt like redemption. He looked me squarely in my face, flopped his precious cap on my damp head, and flashed me that adorable toothy smirk. The tightness in my throat relaxed. Drawing on my brother's playful spirit, I faced the open bay and turned my back to the city that embraced human oppression.

The water darkened as it deepened beneath our boat. The blood crinkled in my veins. The joy on my brother's face encouraged me for the next leg of our adventure. We stayed on the deck, speechless, wide-eyed, and alert, taking every jolt of the waves with new determination. A few miles offshore, the gales of wind that launched us twisted into a violent storm. At times I feared we'd be lost in the Gulf. The sails popped loud as the wind howled against them. We hunkered down as the rain pelted like hens pecking corn.

Mother called to us, waving her arms. We could barely hear her above the sound of the storm. She motioned for us to sit together on opposite sides of an iron pole near the center of the deck. My arms went around my brother and his came around me. We hooked our legs around the pole as we braced against the wind. Mother wrapped herself around the two of us as best she could. We all held tight until the worst of the storm had passed.

Somewhere from his past, Daddy summoned a sense of seamanship. He worked with the crew as if he had been doing it all his life, and together they kept the old boat afloat. He dedicated himself to the work even though the wind burned his face until his skin was cracked and peeling beneath a straggle of beard.

Most among us were retching by the time we saw the shore again. There wasn't much celebration, and there wasn't much to say. We were all just happy to see land. Meals on the schooner were a disgusting bowl of vegetable mush and old bread. No one ate much. Fresh water was limited, and the last day we had none. Mama grew very thin with a regular sickness every morning. Our boat pulled into the Bay of Matagorda with Daddy looking much older than his thirty-three years.

We docked at the Port of Lavaca. It was a fish camp and not much more. Daddy planned to hire a buggy or a wagon to carry us and all our belongings into the frontier, but there weren't any buggies to hire. A man had some horses to sell, but Mother was in no condition to ride a horse. Some of the families commenced walking into Mexico, but Mother wasn't up to it. We'd have to find another way.

The men who crossed the Gulf together felt something of a brotherhood. As good men will do, a small band deliberated among themselves. Within a day, one of them learned of a crumbling flatboat that was available for sale. In short order the men pooled their money, purchased the flatboat, and loaded everyone for the next part of our journey.

For two days, we watched the ripple of murky water as our salvaged craft slipped along the Lavaca River bringing us further into the country. It gave me something of a dizziness, at which time I'd just close my eyes and think of what awaited us—fields of grain, rivers overflowing with fresh fish, and a land so bountiful it brought wealth to one's front door. That was the promise of Mexico.

If New Orleans opened our eyes to America's social differences, the next stop gave me a glimpse of the differences that awaited us in Mexico. The team of men took shifts at the long poles, pushing the flatboat against the current of the river. After forty-eight hours of heavy work, the men stopped in a place called Old Scotts. It was a primitive camp where families could connect with land agents who helped them find the land they wanted in Mexico.

There was a hut where a man stayed alone, greeting folks and asking where they were headed. That was all. There were no tents or buildings for travelers. There was a corral intended for horses. There was an empty hay crib. There were no horses, and no hay. The men from our boat constructed temporary shelters for us out of palmetto palms. They engineered the frame of a large hut using the lumber from the flatboat. I watched in complete amazement as the men cut wide, coarse, emerald branches of the low-growing palmetto. It was nature's perfect umbrella. Scores of palmetto palms were piled over the frame, forming a roof to shed the rain.

The world felt different on this side of the Gulf. The ground was damp, but I didn't see any ice. Some trees were bare, but there were leaves and vegetation on low-growing shrubbery. Winter in Mexico came mildly. I liked that.

While the palmetto shelter was being built, the women began to organize their baggage. A man called to our daddy. The man held a long gun in one hand and the other hand clutched the legs of a large bird, the thing's head dragging the ground. The women took charge of finishing the shelter while the men turned their attention to plucking and cleaning the wild creature to be sacrificed for our supper.

My brother John ran from one place to another. As always, he was driven by his curiosity, and enthralled by his discoveries, but I saw a new anxiety in his eyes. "Did you see that, Syd? We're gonna eat that big bird for supper." He was awestruck, but there was no smile on his face. He shook his hands in nervous jitters. His wide eyes flitted. The strain of our journey, the bad food, lack of sleep, and lack of predictability were taking a toll on us all.

Gradually, I was realizing the reality of our predicament. Was this what our father expected? Was this the way it was to live off the land with only a shelter of palmetto over a dirt floor, eating fresh meat with the victim's blood still on the hunter's clothes?

"Yes, little brother. I saw that big bird. Let's get Mama a place to sleep." Working was a good distraction.

The men created temporary living arrangements for the women and children in one area and the men in another. I hoped it wouldn't stay that way for very long. We sacrificed privacy for security, and I was learning a new meaning of community. Each of four women claimed a sector of our shelter for herself and her children. Our belongings were arranged as a sort of perimeter. Pots, pans, water jugs, cups and platters were stacked at the ready, pretending to be as much of a home as we could arrange. The brotherhood of men stayed together, and they talked business as if there was no time to lose. I overheard a conversation between my daddy and the land agent, Mr. Isaac Deats.

"Now, Davis you can have land right here and you don't have to go any further. You got fishing or you could run a ferry; maybe the missus would like to build another inn, like you had in Kentucky." I thought those were all opportunities my daddy would consider, and for a moment I feared we had found our new home. But I was relieved.

"No, Deats. Rebecca isn't taking to the coastal climate. This is too marshy and damp. I had in mind a good black land farm for row crops," Daddy said. "I would like to go on to the DeWitt settlement."

"Gonzales. Yep, there's been folks there five years now. Okay, then. I'll take you there. We'll start out tomorrow," Deats agreed.

"I'll give Gonzales a fair look. Then we'll see."

The first night came and went with no sleep. There was a lot of groaning and deep sighing. Every time I sat up to look around, someone else was doing the same. We were an anxious group. When I asked about our daddy, Mother simply put her finger to her lips to indicate quiet, so I was.

In those first forty-eight hours, I had a lot of time to think things over. There was a sad contradiction of what I actually saw of Mexico and what I hoped might await us in Gonzales. Surely a town five years old would be a nice place to live; surely as nice as the Green River Inn. At the end of the second day I reminded my mother we needed to learn our Catholic prayers. She smiled and brushed my hair with her hands. The prayers we said that night were our Kentucky Methodist prayers, and I didn't press the point. They seemed good enough for her.

My fears strengthened on the morning of our third day in Old Scotts as I watched my father walk away with Mr. Deats. We were defenseless children with our mothers, enduring our days and nights in a hut made of palmetto palms, in the middle of winter. I wondered if anyone else noticed. My heart was heavy with doubts, but I felt I needed to be grown-up about it.

I resolved to overcome those doubts with determination. I had to believe the family could thrive in the face of whatever challenges came our way, so long as we had love and each other. I reasoned that the palmetto hut was adequately comfortable, and we were left well-fed. We were fortified with the bundles and pro-visions we had carried down two rivers and across the Gulf of Mexico. I settled into our temporary shelter, holding onto a thread of confidence. Daddy was off with a promise to return before we could miss him.

The first day without our daddy passed slowly. I often found myself glancing down the road that took him away. John and I as-sumed responsibility for ourselves and Mama, very aware that this was more responsibility than we ever had before. Planning seemed appropriate. We sat outside the palmetto hut on two fallen trees.

"Well, here we are little brother. This is Mexico. What do you think?"

John was quiet, chewing on a thick shaft of grass. "I don't know, Sydna." He shook his head and looked around us. "Maybe I'll think better of it all tomorrow." John looked sad, which was totally out of his character.

Finally, when the light of day slid away, we made our place for the night under the covers of our temporary bed. After a long while, as no sleep was coming, I ventured an almost silent inquiry.

"John," I whispered under the covers. "Are you awake?"

"Yeah, I am. And I'm scared." There was a long, awkward pause. My brother would never have admitted fear in the daylight.

Finally, I allowed myself to acknowledge what I heard. "Me, too, Johnny. But we can't let on to Mama."

Bundled in the bedding together, we covered our heads and snuggled so close we shared our breath.

"This is no time to be scared, John. Let's just make the best of this. You stick with me real close, and we'll get through one day at a time until Daddy comes back."

My brother sighed deeply. He wasn't one to cry, but I could sense distress emanating from his skinny body. He didn't have much to say, but silent concerns filled the space under our blanket.

"Syd?"

"Yeah?"

"How 'bout we say that prayer. You know, the one about the valley of death. Okay?"

"Sure, little brother."

I reached for his hands, and realized he was shaking. In the darkness we repeated the words as best we could remember.

"The Lord is my shepherd. I shall not want. He makes me to lie down in green pastures. He leads me beside still waters."

We were both suddenly aware of the imagery of the words. Green pastures; still waters; the elements of our present surroundings. The irony of their significance in our current situation silenced us momentarily. Then I said the next line.

"Yea, though I walk through this valley, under the shadow of death, I will fear no evil."

My brother's hands squeezed mine, and I heard him stifle his gentle sobs.

I continued without him. "You, God are with us. Your rod and staff will comfort us. You are preparing a table for us. Our cup will run over."

I took a deep breath as my fingers felt his release. My brother wiped the tears from his face and joined me in the last words of assurance.

"Surely goodness and mercy will follow us all the days of our life. May we dwell in the house of the Lord forever."

In the darkness my brother turned away from me, rolling his legs up until his body made a little ball. He pulled our blanket back from his head and took in a staggered breath. He sniffed and rubbed his face with the covers.

We were quiet. I waited to hear if my mother had awakened. The camp was filled with the night sounds of locusts and toads. Nature's song grew louder. The nearby riverbed gurgled. Rain splattered against the fronds overhead. An owl hooted, and a breeze whistled through the trees. But there were no other voices.

"Syd?"

"Yeah?"

"I feel better."

We both did. I closed my eyes and slept.

February 20, 1831 – Mama Reveals her Secret

Daddy was gone to Gonzales to claim his land. While awaiting his return, for the first time in my life at the age of thirteen, I felt I was in charge. It was unlike our mother to allow me this much authority. I wondered if she considered me that grown-up, or if she was making a concession because of our difficult trip. We knew she was ill, and I told myself that was the reason. But I soon learned it was for none of those reasons.

The second morning after Daddy left with Mr. Deats, Mama woke up early, before the other women. She quietly awakened my brother and me. With a smile on her face, she curled her finger as a signal for us to follow her. We sat sleepy-eyed and looked at each other. It was cold. We wrapped together in the blanket we shared, slipped on our shoes, and like Siamese twins joined at the hip we followed her outside. Mother took a long slender stick in her hands and gestured for us to sit on the tree trunk as she stoked the fire from simmering coals. She drew herself full height, took a deep breath, and took a seat near John. We all looked into the infant flames as they grew to warm us.

"Children, we need to have a talk," she said. She put the stick beside her, leaned a bit forward, and intertwined her fingers in front of her. Then she was quiet.

"Yes, Mama," we replied in chorus, wondering what on earth this could mean.

"You children are growing up. I can see how responsible you are, and I want you to know how proud I am of you."

We waited. "Yes, ma'am."

"Sydna, you're keeping up with things in here a lot better than I can. John, you're sometimes bringing in food to help the whole camp. Why, you children are doing a grown man's work and a grown woman's work."

We waited again. "Yes, Mama."

She got up and walked a step toward the fire. She poked at the fire with the stick. We all continued to stare at the flames in the brief silence as she sat down.

"So, I guess you're old enough to know that I … I'm really depending on you now." Her voice broke, tears filled her eyes, and her lip began to quiver. "I don't want to, but I need to rest."

She took the corner of her wide sleeve and dabbed at her nose.

John turned toward her and said, "Ma, we know you have the rheumatism, and you have a hard time. We want to do our part now."

"Bless you," she said as she reached for his hand. I noticed how big John's hands had grown, and how small Mother looked sitting next to him. I sat quietly, trying to gather my thoughts, wondering what more to say.

"Children, the rheumatism is greatly bothersome, and I'm hoping in the summer to overcome it. But by summer our family will be different."

Another silence. We couldn't guess what she was thinking.

"What I need you to know is I have a baby in here." She rubbed her belly.

Before I could stop myself, I threw off my corner of the quilt and jumped from the log. "Oh, Mama, does Daddy know?"

Mama laughed. She put her fingers to her mouth and bid me shush a bit, so as not to wake the other women. "Yes, I told him our first night at the hotel in New Orleans."

Images from the past flashed through my mind. The years at home with Susie and John were precious, and I hoped we might live that way again with another baby.

"Mama, you need rest. Now, don't you worry about anything. John and me, we'll do all the work, and you just rest."

I looked at my brother who seemed relieved at the news, glad it wasn't something worse.

Two other women appeared from the palmetto leaves. "Are ye'aw okay?"

"Yes, we're fine," Mama said.

I wanted to shout out about the baby, but I caught myself before I blurted it out. John looked at me, and we both laughed.

"Well, let's get the coffee started," Mama said. And our day began.

February 23, 1831 – Sandhill Cranes

We quickly fell into a routine that worked well for all of us in the camp. We conserved our supplies, but encouraging words cost us nothing, so we used them freely. We exaggerated our expressions of hope and joy just to maintain a positive atmosphere. We knew it was all in our heads, but we enjoyed a feeling of being responsible, believing we could cultivate courage just by our conversations.

"Good morning, Mama. How beautiful you look today. John, doesn't Mama look beautiful?"

"She sure does. Mama, you're the prettiest woman in these parts." John would give her a kiss on the cheek.

Mama played our positivity game with us. "Well, you children make me proud, and proud is beautiful."

"I bet Daddy is missing us and thinking about us today. Maybe he'll be back tomorrow. What do you think, Syd?"

"I know he's missing Mama and wanting to be back here just as soon as he can."

We went on like that all day long.

Old Scotts was a well-known camp for immigrants, traders, and folks heading in and out of Mexico. There was a constant hum of activity going on down at the river crossing. We thought it was better than a play on a New York City stage. John and I went to the ferry landing as often as we could just to see the interesting boats and people coming and going. Gradually we ventured off a ways, following the clearing of the river bank beyond the landing and away from the clamor of the people. There was a wide sand bar at a turn in the river. On any sunny day the ground seemed alive with wiggly river bugs making their way across the wet sand. John wanted to get crawfish out of the little mounds of mud.

One day we went there and were treated to a rare sight. Secluded just enough not to be disturbed by the hustle of the ferry landing was a flock of tall birds. There were hundreds of them, dressed in light gray feathers. Silently, we settled on the edge of the woods and watched. My brother poked me with his elbow, pointing with one hand to his head. A distinctive cap of red feathers crowned each of their heads.

These were the sandhill cranes, just ending their winter stay on the Gulf. They chortled and chuckled their friendly coos, shaking their bills at their companions, totally unaware of our existence. Tucked into the brush, we settled in to enjoy the spectacle.

To our good fortune, we discovered them in the last hours of their stay. They were excited. As time went by, their tension increased. Suddenly, they all turned as if it had been planned all along. Nature whispered. They knew it was time for their departure. They bent their legs in unison and leapt from the sand. Water sprinkled from their bodies and glistened as the droplets fell back to earth. Flying close together, they appeared as one being. Like a tapestry being lifted from the wash, they swooped up together and were off to the north. They called to each other in the excitement of the moment, as they spread their wings and gracefully left us.

Something spoke to my soul in the moments I sat in wonder watching them leave. They had each other, and they had their independence. They had the whole span of heaven, and they could each go their own way if they chose to. But when the cycle of life called on them to move along into their future, they all remained with the flock. That was like us. I glanced through the trees in the direction of our camp and was warmed by the assurance of the flock that waited there for me.

"Let's get back, little brother," I said. And he agreed.

As we entered the camp, Mother shouted to us. "Look what I have!" She waved a crumpled paper. "A letter from your father!"

When we reached her, she read it to us. He wrote:

We made our claim, and you will not be disappointed! We'll have a lot in town for our own home, and we'll grow crops out from town in the fields. I'll be back for you just as soon as I can get there.

In early March, at the end of a day filled with honey-scented air, we were sitting by the evening fire when there was a noise of campers coming up from the ferry. We turned in that direction and strained our eyes to see if it could be our beloved daddy. It was! There he stood, dirty and exhausted. He was grinning from ear to ear. Behind him were a buckboard and a mule.

Mama ran to Daddy as well as she could, and he caught her in his arms. John and I took the reins of the mule and looked him over. We gave that animal the best welcome we could. We rubbed him down, and John brought him some water in a pan.

"He's beautiful," John said. The animal's huge eyes were stunning, all dark and moist like peeled black plums. His lashes were long and thick, like a paint brush with half of the bristles gone. He was a young mule, playfully nudging my brother. He rubbed his gray velvet muzzle against John's shoulders.

"I bet he's hungry," John said to Daddy.

"No, son. This animal is amazing. He's not a race horse. He just paces himself. Sometimes I swear he's thinking about everything around him. He just doesn't eat much. Take him out for a walk in the grass and let him eat a little, but you'll see. He just doesn't eat much. Walk him out there and decide what we're going to call him."

John and I took that mule and walked him like a pet. We missed the horses then and remembered our uncle's farm. We hoped some horses were in our future, but the handsome young mule brought back the joy we had in Kentucky. John decided to call the mule Barley. He said it was kind of like barely needing any food, and barley was a good food for mules. So from that day our family mule was called Barley.

Everyone wanted to hear the stories of Gonzales. The whole camp sat up late that night around the fire, like one big family. It was then I realized that my daddy commanded respect and captivated the attention of our community. They clung to his every word.

For two days, a little crowd of campers took in what Daddy had to tell. It seemed Gonzales might fulfill his needs. Others were also inclined to settle in Gonzales because of what my daddy had to tell. He was exhilarated by the promise of it all, and we caught his enthusiasm. When he was sufficiently rested, we loaded Mother in the back of the buckboard. Daddy made her a soft place to sit so she could lean against the bundles as we went along. John and I sat on either side of our father, and we started back along the trail into the heart of Tejas.

Part 2:

Life in the Promised Land

March 5, 1831 – Welcome to Gonzales

On a clear March morning, Barley pulled our buckboard into Gonzales.

"This is your new home, my dear." Daddy winked at Mama. He reached over to my brother, lifted his cap, and plopped it back down onto John's head.

John adjusted the cap and watched as Daddy got down to lead Barley up the road. We were passing into our promised land. We were no longer travelers. We were settlers.

The cedar elms greeted us with tiny sprouts of green on the branches. We went through the little square lots until we reached a dirt road clearly marked Water Street. Our first sight of the town proved it to be something more than Old Scotts camp, but I quickly realized this was not Green River, Kentucky. We would have no polished floors or cushions on our furniture for a while.

Eight cabins were sprinkled across the lots that defined the perimeter of town. The streets were mud with ruts clearly marking the tracks where wagon wheels rolled. The cabins were rough, wooden structures with leather hides over the windows. Some cabins had a door while others had only an opening where a door should be. There was no paint, no brick, and no glass windows.

We led Barley up Water Street to a two-story building with a sign marked HOTEL. Daddy went inside. In a moment, he returned with Mr. Tom Miller, the town official who kept records for the Mexican government. He asked Daddy a lot of questions, like

"Where did you come from?" and "How long you been traveling?" He wanted to know if any of us were sick. He made some notes on a paper, and he never asked if we were Catholic.

"Well, Davis, let's go see that lot you picked out. I think it's one of the best." He walked ahead of the wagon, up a street marked St. Louis. We'd barely gone a half block when he stopped. He turned to the buckboard, took Barley's rein, smiled at us, and said, "This here is yore home. Welcome to Gonzales, neighbors." With a swoop of his hand and a slight bow, he gestured to the lot behind him.

Mama stood up and looked around. Daddy came to help her off the buckboard. John and I climbed down from the seat.

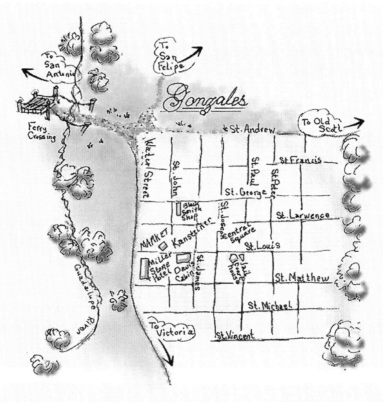

Map of Gonzales, 1835

As I came down from the buckboard, Mr. Miller took my hand and smiled at me. "Hello, young lady." He removed his hat and looked at me like I was somebody important. It reminded me of the day Joshua Morgan first looked at Susie. We all stood quietly, looking over our property.

So, this is to be our home—a square lot of dirt, within sight of a river, I thought. I looked back at Mr. Miller, and he tipped his hat, sort of rocking on his boots.

John took off his cap and looked the place over. He squatted down and sat on his left heel. A large, bare tree with rough, peeling bark towered near the center. A few patches of weeds grew on little muddy hills in between puddles, but nothing else lived on the place. Daddy walked to the tree and put his left hand on it.

"That's a pecan tree." Mr. Miller looked up into the branches. "You'll have a good crop come fall."

Daddy looked up into the tree to acknowledge Mr. Miller's words. He removed his hat with his right hand and faced the interior of his lot, lost in his imagination. We all stood quietly. Mother's lip quivered as she cupped her chin in her right hand, her left hand supporting her elbow. She turned her head away to quiet a deep sigh. I leaned my head on her arm and stayed quiet, respecting the soberness of the moment.

Mr. Miller broke the silence. "You folks come stay a night at my hotel, and we'll start you a shelter tomorrow."

Mama made a pleading look as Daddy approached her. He quickly agreed to accept the kind offer and led us all back onto the buckboard. Daddy helped Mama as she struggled to get back into the buckboard. He turned Barley around slowly, and we made our way back toward Water Street.

"Get yore missus settled, and I'll show you around town," Mr. Miller said.

We took Mama to the hotel. At the edge of the street, a single step led up to a boardwalk which ran along Water Street.

The boardwalk became a long, broad porch in front of the hotel. As we entered the hotel, a small, energetic young woman greeted us from behind the bar. Mr. Miller introduced her as Anita.

"Welcome to Gonzales," she said with great enthusiasm and a heavy Spanish accent. She wore a white blouse with sleeves that gathered just above her elbows. It dipped slightly at the neck revealing beautiful brown skin. Her full skirt was made up of bright red and yellow triangles falling just below her knees. She wore flat leather shoes that wrapped around her feet and tied at her ankles.

Mother sat in the chair Anita brought to her, and they smiled at each other. Anita tossed a mass of her black hair off her shoulders to settle it behind her back. "Now, you just go. You do what you need to do. Mama stays here for a rest." And she stood with her hands on her hips behind Mama's chair.

"You heard the lady!" Mr. Miller said. "Let's go see your town." With that, he led us out of the hotel. John snapped both his hands in front of him, letting off some nervous energy. We walked down to the corner of Water Street, turned the corner, and continued up the street marked St. Louis. We walked past our own lot and up two more blocks.

The town was laid out in a large square with seven lots on each street—seven lots going east to west, and seven lots going north to south. Water Street was the outer edge of town on the west side. Lots were granted first from the outside edge of town, moving inward as more folks claimed them. From the town center, we could see all the way back to Mr. Miller's hotel. The whole town seemed not much bigger than the whole of our place at the Green River Inn.

"This here is our new courthouse," Mr. Miller explained as we stood in the center of the town. There was a wooden structure where three men were closing in a roof. "In this square here we generally get together like folks did when you were here before. We like to come here in the evenings and just sit a while, talking things over. We'll have a church over there on that corner, and the school is goin' in over there." He pointed to various empty lots.

Crossing half of Gonzales reminded me of the mornings we ran to Uncle Thomas's barn. It seemed to me the town lots were mighty small compared to our home in Kentucky. If this was the promise of Mexico, I was beginning to feel disappointed.

"This is what I was trying to describe to your mother," Daddy explained. "I met some nice folks here, and they'll be good friends."

Along the path to the construction site of the courthouse, I saw the low circular stone wall of a firepit. In the center of the pit sat the large knot of a tree trunk, blackened from recent flames. Stumps of trees were arranged around the outside of the firepit, as if designed for folks to sit a while. The scene gave evidence of being used for a gathering.

"We'll come back later this evening. I'd like to see some of those men I met before," Daddy said.

I thought Daddy was trying to calm John's nervous jitters.

"What's that?" John asked, pointing to a small wooden building with boarded-over windows.

"That there is the jail, young man. And then there's the blacksmith shop. Behind the smith is a wheelwright. We can take care of most anything folks need," he said. "We had a good start on the town back in '25, but the Indians burned it down in '26. They caught us off guard, and they came in while most of the town folks were away."

I didn't say anything, but I'm sure Mr. Miller saw a look of shock on my face.

"More people are here now, so we don't worry about that so much anymore. We started rebuilding after the raid, and we're more civilized now."

John glanced over at me with the corners of his mouth pulled stiff in a concerned look as he pulled his elbows in against his ribs and brought his fists together in front of him.

What I saw was not what I would consider a town. It was a long, long way from what I thought of as civilized. There were canvas tents and grass huts like what we had in Old Scotts. Partial structures appeared on scattered town lots, and some temporary huts were on the prairie beyond the town.

After a brief guided tour of the community, we made our way back to Mr. Miller's hotel. We walked on the long, covered porch. From the porch, we could enter either of two doors—one marked GENERAL STORE and the other marked TAVERN. Both doors led into the same building marked HOTEL where Mother was waiting with Anita.

"Let me help you with your bags, Mr. Davis."

Daddy instructed us to stay with Mama while he and Mr. Miller brought in our things.

"Let's get your Mama settled in a room and then if you want to, we can go back outside for a while."

"Now you can rest in here," Anita said kindly as she opened the door to our room. "I'll bring Mama some water." She took the big pitcher from inside the wash basin sitting on a table, and she disappeared.

We settled Mama into a chair, and she propped her feet on the bed.

"Help me get these shoes off."

"Yes, Mama," John said.

He took her left foot between his knees and pulled. Kerplop. The left shoe went to the floor. He tugged the other shoe off and tossed it beside the first. Her feet were so swollen her toes looked like peas bulging out from their pods.

Anita came back with the pitcher full of water and a soft cloth over her arm. "I'll help your mama now. You two go explore the town." She poured a pool of water into the wash basin and set the pitcher on the floor next to Mama's shoes. Then she dipped the soft cloth into the water and rung it out to dampness. She motioned to us to go.

I looked at Mama, and she nodded to the door. I walked with my little brother toward the hall. Before I closed the door, I glanced back into our room. Anita was rubbing Mama's feet with the damp cloth. Mama eyes were closed, and her lips were curled up in a slight smile. John and I went downstairs to meet our daddy.

"Let's go see our town," Daddy said.

We took a walk all around the town, just getting a sense of Gonzales. Folks were friendly enough. I looked forward to knowing their names, knowing where they lived, and knowing how we would fit in.

Sure enough, as the sun began to hide behind the tree line, half a dozen or so people gathered near the construction site of the new courthouse. They tipped their hats and nodded their heads in greetings, and we nodded back.

"Hey, Davis. I see you come on back." The greeting came from one of the men making a small fire in the stone pit.

"Hey, there, Dan. Good to see you again. These are my children, Sydnie and John."

I nodded to the man and tucked myself under my daddy's arm. John stepped forward, reached out his hand, and the man named Dan shook it gently.

"Fine family you got, Davis."

Daddy told him about our trip from Old Scotts. He explained that Mama was waiting for us in the hotel and that we needed to get back to her.

I suddenly felt tired and ready to end our first day in Gonzales.

"Come eat some chili," Anita offered as we came into the hotel for the last time.

"Now, that's awful generous of you," Daddy said.

"You one of us now, Davis," Mr. Miller said. "Might as well start out right. Nita's chili is about as good as it gets 'round these parts. We'll set you up a table for the family."

We went to our room to get Mama.

"George, I can't get my feet back into those shoes," Mama said when we told her about supper downstairs.

"I think you can go down in your bare feet," Daddy said.

"No, George, I can't go down there barefoot. Maybe you can bring me something up here."

"You just wait one minute and let me see what I can do. You children come downstairs with me."

Daddy showed us to a table in the tavern and told us not to budge. We wouldn't dare in this new place. Daddy went to the kitchen. Together, the three of them—Anita, Mr. Miller, and Daddy—slipped around the various rooms for several minutes. Then Daddy went upstairs with a bundle in his hands. In a few minutes he appeared again, grinning. He had Mama by the arm, and she looked happier than she had since we left Kentucky. As she made her way down the steps, she lifted her long skirt and I could see she was wearing a pair of beautiful, flat, leather slippers. They were just like the ones Anita wore.

"These shoes are marvelous," she whispered as she slid into a chair next to me.

We sat in the tavern till after dark, eating chili that lingered on our tongues long after it was swallowed. Folks came and went, and Mr. Miller seemed to have something for everyone—a paper to sign, a sack of meal, or a drink from behind the long, wooden bar. Finally, we made our way to our room for the night.

"George, where are the thousands of acres you're supposed to get?" Mama asked as we were getting ready to sleep.

"Well, dear, I have a plan for that. You see, I can save some money by making a partnership. That way I get help with the upfront cost and then help with the planting. There's a man by the name of Nash who wants to go in by halves. I thought that would be just the thing. Maybe I'll find time to cure some pelts, and I can get set up for making boots." Suddenly, he had an idea, and his face lit up with the excitement of it. "In fact, maybe I'll make some of those comfortable shoes you liked so much." He smiled at Mama. "I'll be working on all that, don't you worry."

"That makes sense," she said in a tired voice. She pulled the covers over John. "We'll talk about it tomorrow." She lay down and went to sleep.

The day after we arrived in Gonzales, a small crew of men met Daddy on our town lot. They began another temporary shelter for our family. First, they brought freshly cut saplings from the river. They leaned long slender saplings together to make a frame. A grass hut similar to the shelter in Old Scotts began to appear. John and I watched from the single window of our hotel room.

"What are they doing out there, children?" Mother asked us from where she lay on the bed.

"Remember Old Scotts?" John asked.

After a long pause, her hoarse voice said, "Yes."

"Well, it's like that," my brother said.

We looked at each other and knew that was as much as she should hear just now.

Mother put one arm over her eyes and sighed. I noticed how very thin that arm had become. Her feet were crossed and hung just beyond the bed covers, and I could see her swollen ankles. *How much more can she take?* I wondered. I stood looking at her, realizing I had never once heard her complain of discomforts. Surely, she missed the inn and longed for Midge's sweet-natured companionship. I wished Susie was here with us and wondered what she was doing. I was sure Mama felt the same, but if Mama wouldn't mention it, I knew I shouldn't either.

March 8, 1831 – The Kansteiners

The Kansteiner family lived across the street from our lot on St. Louis Street. There were three members of the family—Copper and Els'beth Kansteiner and their daughter, Julia. They were among the first to arrive and had been there for the full five-year duration of the town. During those five years, they had completed their home, built a large barn, and become pillars of the community. They were hard workers and dedicated any spare time to helping others. Mr. Kansteiner organized the group to build our shelter.

Julia was something of a ten-year-old stinker. She had a stand-offish way that, at first, appeared to be shyness. In spite of her efforts to attempt subtlety, she had a devilish streak she couldn't hide for long.

On the day her father headed up the team of men building our shelter, she stood at the road with her thumb in her mouth, just watching. When the men took a break from their work, Julia ran to the place and began removing the limbs they had assembled. It must have been a very awkward episode for Mr. Kansteiner, who simply walked his daughter from the worksite to her own house across the street. He disappeared into his house and in a very few minutes reappeared through his front door. Without much concern, the crew of men just replaced the limbs and continued working as if nothing had happened at all.

My dumbfounded brother looked at me and exclaimed, "Dang!"

We both knew we would never get away with such sabotage, nor would we want to. We snickered at the unexplainable behavior. I put a finger to my puckered lips to remind John to keep things quiet for Mama.

"What's going on out there?" Mama wanted to know.

"Nothing, Mama. They're just building us a shelter. It's nothing."

Mama made a long sigh and turned her back to us.

When Daddy came in for the evening, John couldn't contain his curiosity. "Why did she do that, Daddy? Why did she undo all your work?"

"Son, the girl has been through some trouble. She's not right," Daddy said.

John just looked at me again with that tight-lipped expression of his. The subject of Julia Kansteiner was closed, and we went to the town center to meet up with new neighbors at the firepit.

As the months went by, we made our way through each day scavenging for food and trying to learn what this new life required. We had staples from New Orleans, but we knew they wouldn't last long. We learned to trap, hunt, and gather plants from the woods. The propaganda Daddy read about living off the land was true, but no one had warned us of the dangers.

For every good gift of nature there was a risk. There *were* fish in the streams, but beside the stream was the itch vine. The first spring we spent some miserable days with oozing blisters. There *was* wild vegetation, but the dappled copperhead lived under the leaves. A rattler might be sunning itself near an outcropping of stones, or possibly hunting a rat near last year's woodpile. There was much to learn if we were to achieve what we envisioned.

We were truly ignorant of what it would take to survive in Mexico. Every day was another lesson, and we learned by listening. We learned about nature and about the Indians. Our neighbors shared what they knew, and I respected their counsel.

The mornings started at sunrise with the smell of coffee across the town. It was truly community as everyone encouraged each other, helped each other, supported each other, and advised each other. When the sun began to set in the west, most town folks migrated toward the community fire right there in the middle of town, just as Mr. Miller told us they would. The firepit was just a few short blocks from our lot, as near as Uncle Thomas had been in Kentucky. Our new neighbors shared their stories and sometimes food. Men and women offered help where it seemed needed, and the bonds of friendship tightened. We all needed each other, and we knew it.

After Mama recovered some from the trip, she came with us to the evening gatherings at the town campfire. She met the ladies in town, and she especially liked Mrs. Els'beth Kansteiner. They felt an instant kinship. Mama learned of the dreadful memories Julia carried in her head. With great sadness in her voice, Mama explained what happened.

"I can't imagine the suffering these people have been through," she began. "That poor Julia, she'll never be right. Her mama can barely keep a straight mind." Mama shook her head as she put a towel around the handle of a pot of beans and removed it from the fire next to our thatched shelter. She put the pot on the ground to cool, and she sat down on one of the tree stumps we used for a bench.

"Back in July of '26, the town folk went over to Columbus, another settlement quite a ways off, to celebrate the fiftieth year of America's Independence. It was the older Kansteiner boy who organized it all. I think his name was Eugene. They planned to stay on the road for a whole week. The more the town talked about it, the more people wanted to go. They'd all been working so hard, and they had just built their homes and all."

Mama pulled at the hair that fell in her face, tucked it behind her ear, and looked at the Kansteiner place across St. Louis Street. "When it was time to go, the Kansteiner boy took sick. He ran a terrible fever and couldn't get out of bed. The rest of the people went, even Copper. But Els'beth and her boy stayed behind."

Mama stirred the beans with a big spoon she brought from Kentucky. She looked around at the mud on our lot and tapped the spoon on the edge of the pot. With the saddest tone I ever heard in her voice, she finished the story. "A band of Comanche came in here, George. Right here, on this lot."

Daddy was sitting on a log, whittling on a stick and listening. He stabbed his knife into the log and tossed the whittled piece to the side. "Rebecca, I know it was a terrible thing," he said as he leaned on his elbow in her direction. "But there are more people coming now, and things are safer."

Mama ignored his words. "Els'beth said they were quiet; they didn't whoop like Indians usually do. But she heard the ponies on the road, and she heard them splash in the river. She was in the yard when she heard them, and she thought it was someone from town coming home. When she saw who it really was, it was too late. She couldn't get into the house, so she ran to the barn. George, you know she couldn't help her son. She wanted to, but she couldn't. They scalped him, George. And then they set the rest of the town on fire." Mama's voice was pleading, wanting to justify a mother who made the desperate decision to abandon her son in his sick bed. "Some things are impossible," she said as she stirred the beans again, big tears running down her cheeks.

Daddy told the rest of the story. "The town folk—those who went to Columbus—they saw the smoke at a distance and guessed what happened. They got help and came back home, but it was too late. Julia ran into the house and found her brother, all blood-soaked in his bed. Mrs. Kansteiner was still hiding in the loft of the barn, too afraid to go back to the house. Copper told us about it." Daddy finished the Kansteiner story.

And then there was more about the Indians.

The crew of men building our cabin had told Daddy what they knew from their experiences. The Indian practice was to lay siege to a town, take what they wanted, burn what they left, and leave the scalped victims as a sign of their power. Finding the town empty must have appeared easy pickings for the Comanche that July day. They found no resistance at all. Taking the scalp of a desperately ill young man seemed to me the lowest of corruptions. They burned everything else in town, but for some reason they did not burn the Kansteiner's house and barn. That was amazing. The only family in town whose property survived the raid carried the violence in their hearts. Julia was left not right, and Els'beth was a nervous wreck. The Kansteiners emerged as a sort of sacred family, respected for their courage to rise above their loss.

It was months before I began to sleep at night. At first, the unfamiliar shrieks in the dark inspired images in my head of savages with blood dripping from their hands. But in time, I was able to identify the hoot of an owl and the bark of a coyote. I could identify the passion of a rabbit's death squeal from the distant woods. Eventually I learned the sounds that meant all was well. The locust song and the deep-throated call of a tree frog confirmed there was nothing going on out there in the dark. When the new and unusual became familiar, my anxieties began to settle down a bit. I started to become a real pioneer girl.

June 1831 – Mariah Dirkson

Winter passed, and the seasons changed. Then in June, on a sultry morning before the sun began to rise, I heard an unidentifiable sound. At first, I thought it was a kitten, lost from its mother. I adored kittens, and I would have been thrilled to rescue one. Maybe I'd have an excuse to bring it home and keep it.

I listened keenly. The piercing squeal just didn't match anything I knew. I wanted to investigate.

The sound came from the direction of the river. I slipped out of our shelter quietly, hoping to coax the kitten to me. I tracked the sound. Yes, it seemed to be coming from the ferry landing, but I wasn't leaving our lot in the dark, barefoot and dressed in my underclothes.

Then, from out of the morning silence I heard the sound of others responding to the squeal.

"Mariah," a neighbor called out in a desperate voice. "It must be Mariah!"

A woman was running up the road yelling her daughter's name. Mariah Dirkson disappeared in the last weeks of 1830. It was all the talk of the town when we first arrived. There were Indians in the woods, and her parents were certain she had been kidnapped. A search party had been looking all that time with no success. But that morning, sure enough, there at the ferry landing on the opposite shore of the Guadalupe was a teenage girl on her hands and knees, breathlessly gasping for help.

Most everyone in town was awake by the time they launched the ferry. They wasted no time getting the Dirksons across the river to bring Mariah home. There was such crying and pleading. Everyone around was overjoyed and horrified, all at the same time. Mrs. Dirkson screamed, at first with delight to see her daughter, and then again in anguish when she saw Mariah's condition.

Mariah's face was disfigured with a pattern cut into her cheeks. Two lines of puckered flesh ran outward from her nostrils across each cheek. Her nose flesh was burned away, and she struggled to breathe. The bottoms of her feet were badly burned, and the flesh was still tender. Mariah had crawled through the underbrush for whatever distance it took her to get back home. She was small, and her size probably served her well in hiding from her captors.

Indians were especially creative in ways to disfigure kidnapped girls. The Comanche celebrated wickedness and took pride in their cruelty. Mariah was a victim for their experimentation. Her nose was gone, and those deep lacerations across her cheeks were almost healed, leaving distinctive scars. Her hands, arms, and legs were scratched, and her clothes were rags. She looked like a wild creature with a head of tangled, matted hair.

Mariah and Julia would be forever tortured by their experiences with Indians. Their torment had a profound impact on the rest of us. Sometimes at night, I put my hands on my nose, trying to imagine what it would be like to live without one. The thought of my brother being scalped sometimes suddenly slipped into my brain. I pinched myself to drive the horrible thoughts away.

I lived in fear for a long time. I kept an eye toward the river, wondering what lurked beyond the wood line. Life in Gonzales could be blatantly cruel. Every day had the potential for a crisis. We learned to live with danger and tried to create security. In those days, I remembered the Green River Inn and wondered why we ever gave it up. I thought about Susie and daydreamed about our past. But then the tasks at hand brought me back to the reality of our lives in Mexico.

Survival was a community process. There was a loyalty that bonded the settlers in good times and bad. It was a loyalty as strong as family, a loyalty that would prove itself many times.

July 1831 – Jessie and the Carters

Compassion in Gonzales was demonstrated in the case of a single citizen named Jessie. I never knew her last name. She was still a child, not yet a teen.

Jessie came to Gonzales with a man who then disappeared and left her behind. No one knew the relationship she had to the man, whether it was her brother, her father, or any other true relative. Maybe he stole her. No one knew. She was an elusive and some-what mysterious little soul, a little ragamuffin who just showed up from time to time and place to place. Life had aged her.

Jessie had the most distinctive face I ever saw on any human. Her eyes were huge. Under each eye was a circle of gray, like she needed sleep. Above each eye was a long, thick row of brow hairs. At some distance, the brows and the circles almost connected, making her look much like an owl. And to make the likeness even stronger, she closed her eyes when she turned her head.

The man who brought Jessie to town had lived in the streets, bathed in the river, and survived by his wits. When he left, Jessie continued the same lifestyle. Her feet and hands were scarred from the cruelty of her rugged life. Most girls in Gonzales wore dresses, but Jessie wore pants rolled up between her ankles and her knees. She had no shoes. Her clothes had long ago lost any distinction and were simply the color of time gone by. Bits of straw clung to her like a scarecrow.

Jessie was seen alone for about a week before we realized the man was gone. When Els'beth asked about her companion, she dropped her head and dragged her bare toe across the dirt in front of her. She had nothing to say about him or his whereabouts.

After dark, Jessie pulled a bundle of hay behind a barrel in the corner of Kansteiner's barn, hiding through the night like a scared rabbit. Despite her nighttime fears, she was out of that barn by daybreak. Mrs. Kansteiner tried to befriend her. Jessie was almost won over until Julia began to scream. That ended the trust.

It was in the gardens that Jessie earned her keep. Jessie could weed and hoe, leaving a clean row before you even knew she was there. She'd find the garden tools and just start to work. Then when discovered, her owl eyes would seek approval. If she sensed disapproval, she ran. If she saw a smile, she knew she had permission to take some food from the rows. She would take just what she needed, and she never needed much.

She might come up to the window of a cabin and peek in. Questions were answered with the shake of her head. She never asked for food, but she never turned it down. Sometimes those who shared a meal were honored to share a bit of conversation with her. Jessie tugged at our hearts. She was fiercely independent and suspicious of others, keeping a guarded distance from folks until they earned her trust.

Jessie was a contradiction, suggesting cruelty and compassion all at once. She was grace wrapped in a cocoon of humility. In spite of her rugged life, she moved with the grace of a princess. When she spoke, it was "Yes, ma'am" or "No, sir." She had dignity and manners. She washed as often as she possibly could. In Jessie's presence, I understood that every life is precious and fragile. She reminded us of how much we needed each other. But she also represented the power of independence and sheer determination.

Everyone in Gonzales made the same deal with Mexico, betting our very lives that our efforts here would pay off. In the interest of survival, our neighbors looked out for each other, and that included Jessie.

While we Davises were making a home and a new life on St. Louis Street, a couple named Carter was living five miles out of Gonzales on their league of land. The Carters and my parents became friends soon after we arrived. Mr. Carter invited us to come fishing on his place, and we gladly accepted the invitation. Oh, my, what a place it was!

Carter land was gently rolling hills of beautiful prairie grass dotted with clusters of oaks and cedar elms. We walked out to the high point where you could see for miles. It was just Mr. Carter and his wife, Shandra, out there. They had no children.

Mrs. Carter asked Mama about the living arrangements of Jessie and that man.

"I never see any man, Shandra. Looks to me like Jessie is just alone in town now. Els'beth tells me Jessie stays alone in their barn at night."

After that, the Carters found more reasons to ride to town. They wanted more information about Jessie.

I believe those Carters must have been eager to rise every morning just to breathe in the morning air and take in the reality of their claim. I imagine that every dusk they must have looked toward the west, thankful and maybe still in awe of their land. The Carters had everything they needed. The only thing missing was a child.

In the lower valley of the Carter place was a cluster of shade trees perfectly situated around a small creek feeding the Guadalupe

River. Nature created an oasis there known in our town as Carter Creek, and that's where we fished. Comanche knew of this creek long before the Carters arrived. The Indians resented the white man claiming it. But claimed it was, as Carter's headright.

"Them Comanch' give me fits since I got here," Mr. Carter explained to us. "I had me some good hounds, but they been mostly killed off now."

So Mr. Carter built himself a protection against the Indians. He built a fence, but not just any fence. The perimeter of his home was surrounded by a towering wall of cedar posts. It could not be breached. No one intruded into his yard since his fence was completed. But Carter's Creek was outside the fence.

Carter believed in helping a neighbor, and a neighbor was anyone needing help. He made a regular practice of greeting travelers down at the watering hole to inquire of their destination and to wish them well. If travelers needed to stay the night before moving on, he would offer his front yard inside the fence as a protected camp. His stories of Indian raids usually convinced the travelers to either shelter in the yard or move on. But in the summer of '31, a band of travelers shrugged off his help and paid dearly.

There was a French trader who came all the way from Louisiana. He arrived at the watering hole to rest his animals and his companions just as the shadows grew long. He had several hired hands helping with his two-wheel carts and mules. They were all headed south into the heart of Mexico in hopes of a big payday. There were barrels of whiskey and a trunk of fabric by the bolt. He had trims for sewing and a bunch of women's fancy hats. One mule was packed with garden tools. He had barrels of nails, hammers, and other useful wares. The mules and carts made considerable racket as they moved down the road.

Carter heard them. He went down to invite them to spend the night inside the protection of his fence. The men laughed and said they hadn't seen any Indians since they left Louisiana, which was incredibly rare. They were convinced the tales of Indians were exaggerations, and they felt safe enough.

Carter pointed out the Comanche Moon already rising in the dusk. "That moon will light up the night, and this here's 'zactly the kinda night they come on ya."

In spite of Carter's reasoning, they could not be moved, so Carter went reluctantly back to his cabin. But Carter had a plan.

The Carters didn't sleep that night. Mr. Carter couldn't let the merchants commit suicide just because they were naive. He made a fire just beyond the merchants' camp, left it unattended, and hid undetected in the brush over by the watering hole.

Late in the night, just as Mr. Carter predicted, a dreaded war whoop came up from the distant tree line. The merchants must have felt the earth shake from the thundering pony hooves as the Comanche raided what they thought was the occupied camp. The Indians were confused by the campfire Carter left burning in the distance. When the Indians went to that fire, Carter led the campers out.

Unfortunately, one of the merchants was too sound asleep. Finally realizing there were two camps, the Indians pounced on the second site before the last man could get out. The others escaped on foot. All else was lost, including mules, carts full of their wares, and one ill-fated soul.

Carter said, "When them savages start to whoop, you know it's all over. They swung them tomahawks and had 'em in no time. They broke into the whiskey, and then they ripped into them carts. They got skunk drunk and staggered around wearing them hats. It's a shame. Ain't no call for all that."

In the early morning light, the rescued merchants watched in disbelief from the Carter's house as the Comanche filed over the hills heading east in two columns. In a drunken stagger, they wrapped themselves in the colorful fabrics, leaving long trains trailing behind them.

Carter counted sixty braves leading six mules loaded down with yet unopened bundles. He and his wife brought the survivors and the corpse into town the next day and reported it with all the details. It was gruesome, a dead man with his scalp sliced off.

This was how we learned about our new life, from the stories of our neighbors. Whether Indians, predatory animals, unfortunate accidents, or poisonous plants, we learned to read the signs. Flocks of buzzards circling overhead, the smell of something rotting, unexpected movements in the brush, or the skeleton of a deer near a pool of water, these were the everyday signs of danger. We learned to read the language of the land. Nature would provide, but she would command our respect.

After the raid, Mrs. Carter had all the sadness she could tolerate. She longed to bring Jessie home and give her the comfort and protection of a real family. But she knew Jessie was untrusting.

Several days after the Indian raid, the Carters came back to town for supplies. They arrived in an empty wagon. Mr. Carter came to talk to the men in town. And they came to adopt Jessie.

Mrs. Carter knew Jessie was suspicious of folks, having been abandoned as she was. But Jessie had come to know Mrs. Carter's faithful concern with every visit to town. That day the Carters brought a bit of bait. Mrs. Carter had a puppy.

Just as Jessie had appeared when the corpse came two days earlier, she appeared in the street at the corner of Mr. Miller's general store where the Carters hitched their wagon. The puppy was tied on a very short rope at the seat where Mrs. Carter waited while Mr. Carter went in for supplies.

When Jessie saw the puppy she couldn't resist. She slowed her steps, but they were destined for the little dog. Mrs. Carter saw her coming and refrained herself as long as she could until Jessie was beside the buggy.

"Hello, Jessie. Would you like to pet my puppy?"

Jessie couldn't take her eyes off the dog. When she touched him, she was smitten. The wiggly gray hound dog licked the dirt on Jessie's face, and she became a child again. She grinned and looked up into the eyes of her new mother. Mrs. Carter helped Jessie slip up into the buggy. She placed the puppy in Jessie's lap, with his long ears drooping below Jessie's knees.

Mr. Carter predicted the events going on in the buggy and bought a little bag of sugar candies just in case he needed it. As he brought the supplies out of the store, his eyes moistened as he witnessed his wife and Jessie engaged in conversation and laughter. It was as if they had been family all along.

Jessie didn't need to pack a bag because she didn't own anything. There was no one she needed to tell about her departure with the Carters because she had no other family. The Carters left town with Jessie riding in the buggy, hugging the puppy, licking a candy stick, and feeling happy for probably the first time in her life.

There were friends in the general store who witnessed this rare and precious event. The story was retold in the town square for days. Those who shared the story were as happy as the Carters that an abandoned child would have a second chance at life. After all, that's what we had all come to Mexico for.

Happy as we were for Jessie and the Carters, my brother and I took heed of the Indian raid at the Carter's fishing hole. We still glanced toward the woods, contemplating our questions about Indians. We would soon have our own personal Indian encounter.

Early September 1831 – A Tonkawa Boy

As we grew into our pioneer life, we began to realize what those advertisements back in Kentucky really meant. This land could provide everything we needed. There was no shortage of food, but we had to work for it. We planted the proper gardens for each changing season, and our tables were richer with each harvest. It was the planting, gathering, and hunting we had to learn. We knew we had to go into the woods, even though there were dangers. Daddy learned from the experienced members of the community that there were ways to minimize the danger. He taught us how to keep quiet and to vary our path often.

During our first six months in Gonzales, my brother and I began to venture out together. We occasionally ventured beyond the safety of town. We always went together, and we always had a clear purpose. The woods along the Guadalupe River quickly became our favorite hunting grounds.

Before we left the cabin, we decided what we wanted. Then we secured the proper weapons for our hunt. We knew whether we wanted a fish from the river, a squirrel from the pecan grove, or maybe a large toad from a familiar patch of mud; in each case, a specific technique would be required. All discussion took place before we left. We learned to be quiet and stealthy. Our facial expressions and hand movements became the quiet language of hunting.

Our courage was tested one unforgettable morning. A short, stocky Indian boy was sitting at the river's edge with his back to us. John saw him first. My brother suddenly put his arm out. It blocked my view, but I knew something dangerous was lurking nearby. I froze. My heart was pounding.

I peeked out just where the last of the branches were cascading overhead, giving us plenty of cover. Then I saw the Indian boy. Our bodies were as still as statues. We spoke with our eyes. I wondered if he could hear our hearts pounding as we made our breathing shallow. Our eyes riveted on him.

The boy was small but muscular. He had a remarkably round head, more round than oval. His hair was parted down the middle and fell just below his ears on each side of his head. He squatted there with his knees poking up almost to his shoulders. A large feather was twisted in his hair, pointing down his back. On the back of his left shoulder was a long scar. The puckered skin looked like it was the result of a knife cut, similar to Mariah's scars.

The day was warm, and he was mostly naked. All he wore was a leather apron tied around his waist, covering his groin and buttocks. In his left hand, he held a slender lance ready to strike. He concentrated on the water. His attention to his task was our greatest advantage. He was so focused he never looked our way. Just as he thrust the lance into the water, a barking dog appeared on the opposite shore.

My attention was drawn away from the boy to the dog. I thought that dog looked straight at me. As I watched the dog, a skunk waddled out of the brush and stood in a clearing. Fortunately the dog turned his attention toward the skunk. His yapping became more intense, which distracted the Indian boy. The skunk lifted his tail and sprayed something that smelled awful. The dog squealed and rolled in the thin grass. He rubbed his face in the mud and went into wild contortions.

Meanwhile, the native boy pulled his lance from the water. A nice, big catfish was on the end of his spear. The proud boy began to congratulate himself in the universal language of enthusiasm. He stood, probably anxious to take his trophy home. Then I realized he was crippled. His right leg didn't straighten when he walked.

The Indian carried the fish on his lance. As he walked away, he picked up a leather bag sitting on the ground. He held the lance, the fish, and the leather bag in his hands and put a leg into the brush. Out slid a canoe. In spite of his crooked leg, he easily loaded himself and all his things into the little boat and paddled across the river. The little dog stopped yelping and jumped into the boat. They left and never noticed us.

We sat in the brush like two stones in the landscape, daring not even to breathe. I wondered if there were adults hunting with him. We waited quietly for the ripple of the boat and the whining of the dog to fade. Long after the youth left, we continued to be still. We rolled our eyes as far as we could to see each other and the woods around us.

When John felt it was safe to move, he nodded towards town. He backed down into the shallow thicket that ran along the Guadalupe and crawled on his belly to the edge of Water Street. Then he stood and looked back into the woods. When I saw he was safe, I crawled through the brush and ran as fast as I could to where John waited.

"Aw, man. That was close," we agreed.

That very evening, we confessed our encounter to our daddy and his friends back in town at the community fire. A man called Chockow was at the gathering. He was old and a highly respected member of the community.

"You seen a Tonkawa, I dare say. Indian young'uns not like you," he said. "They take a notion to go do somethin', they just go do it. If he's crippled like you say, maybe he just wants to prove himself. And if he brings home that fish, it makes his family proud." Old Chockow spit out some tobacco juice and wiped his chin.

My brother looked at Daddy. "I guess that's why they call 'em braves."

"Them Tonkawa come 'round ever once in a while." The grizzled man crossed his arms over his chest and pointed his chin to the east of town. "They don't bother us much. They been curious 'bout settlers since we first came out here. Probably harmless, but best you be on the watch."

The old man took a pipe out of his waistband. He bent down and picked up a small twig. He put the twig in the fire and used it to light his pipe. His white hair was long and thin. His cheek bones were high, and his face was deeply tanned. "The red man knows these woods better than we ever can," he said as he winked at John.

He moved the pipe out of his mouth and tapped it on a stone next to where he stood. For a long moment, everyone was quiet. In a voice that sounded like authority, the old man gestured to the group around him. "We here came late to this land. That boy was doing what his people have been doing for centuries." He looked back at John. "Today you had a look back into history."

When Mr. Chockow looked down at my brother, I felt a chill go up my back, but my shoulders shivered it away. Daddy lightened the tone. He pulled the red cap down over John's eyes. "You just mind yourself and do like you did today. Keep your wits about you, and you'll do fine." Daddy looked at the old man as if regarding his wisdom.

The old man put his pipe back in his mouth. He crossed his arms across his chest, pulled his lips into a half smile around the mouthpiece, and held the pipe with his teeth.

I imagined the Indian boy back in his tent with his family. Were his parents proud of him when he presented his fish? Surely Indian families were not so different from my own. I wondered if such a boy could grow up to be a warrior, and maybe take someone's scalp.

Late September 1831 – Eugene is Born

The two facts of our new life muddling my head were dirt and fear. Being dirty and being afraid replaced the sense of peace and security I had in Kentucky. We knew the Green River Inn was safe in the dark, with the windows latched and the door bolted. Living in a grass hut was both dirty and dangerous. I began to wish I could just have a good bath with some sweet-smelling soap.

I suspected my mother felt the same frustrations. She would never complain, but she did like soap. She asked the other Gonzales ladies about it. We were coached on the methods of soap-making. Neighbors shared their soap with us until we could make our own.

Dust from the ash bin and lard from the hogs, that became our soap. We kept a small barrel of the gooey stuff by the wash basin. If we mixed a portion of the wet soap with some salt and dried the liquid in a flat baking pan, it could be broken into bars. That stuff would take the hair off a hide, and it nearly took my hide off. But it was all we had. As Mother's delivery time approached, I thought a lot about how that would happen out here in the wilderness, exposed to nature without a way to get clean.

Mother didn't ask for much, but she was pressing Daddy to complete a more secure home before the baby came. In July, Daddy began to give real serious attention to the cabin. The Kansteiner family had a barn full of cured wood just across the road from our property.

"We'll use that wood out of my barn," Copper told Daddy. "It needs to come out, and then we can put up some more for the next family who needs help."

To get a supply of wood for a cabin, whole trees were cut down in the woods. The men trimmed off the branches and carried the long trunks into the barn on a skid. Then they shaved off the bark and squared-up the trunks using a broad axe. Shingles were cut from the tree trunks and laid out to cure for a while.

Our foundation was set up by the end of July. Then a group of men came every day to raise the walls. They dragged the beams over from the barn and notched the corners. The cabin began to take shape. Mud was slathered in between the beams and they poked moss into the mud. Shingles sealed the roof, and our home was complete by mid-September.

The cabin had two rooms facing each other. One room was for cooking and eating. We all slept in the other room. The floor made a porch between the two rooms, all under one good roof. There was one window opening in each room.

Daddy put special effort into making our doors, which opened out onto the porch. The doors were split across the middle.

They could be closed entirely, or we could close only the bottom half, leaving the top half open for ventilation.

The porch between the two rooms was locally known as a trot, because dogs, cats, kids, and horses trotted out there. Daddy built a heavy table and two broad benches for the trot, which served us well every day we lived on St. Louis Street.

Late in the afternoon on a day in the last week of September, I was on the trot washing shirts on the scrub board. Daddy and John had gone to the fields with Mr. Nash.

All of a sudden, Mama called to me in a panic. "Go get Mrs. Kansteiner."

I looked through the opening of the door to the cooking room. Mama was bent over the table holding her belly.

I went for Mrs. Kansteiner, who came back with me immediately. As we stepped up onto the trot, we heard a baby crying in the sleeping room. Mother had delivered the baby herself.

"You go get some water," Mrs. Kansteiner told me. "Start a fire and stay outside until I call for you."

First, I started a good fire. Then I dipped some water into the kettle and put it on the campfire. I watched for bubbles in the water and waited until Mrs. Kansteiner came out.

She soon appeared with the soiled sheet from Mama's big bed and the wash basin from our sleeping room. "Is the water hot?" she asked.

"Not yet," I said. "No bubbles."

The wash basin was full of bloody stuff that looked like a skinned squirrel. With her strong hands, Mrs. Kansteiner tore the sheet. She took the soiled part of the sheet and laid it on the ground by the campfire. Then she dumped the bloody mass into the soiled sheet and put the whole thing in the fire. We waited for the water to boil.

"You have a little brother now," she said. "I think they're fine." She took the drinking ladle and scooped up some of the simmering water. "It's hot enough."

She put the hot water into the wash basin, swooshed it around, and threw the bloody wash water into the dirt way at the back of our lot. She put two more ladles of hot water into the clean wash basin. Mrs. Kansteiner scrunched the clean fabric and dipped a wadded corner into the hot water.

"Bring me some soap," she said. I brought her the chunk of soap I was using for washing the shirts. She pulled a bit of fabric up, scrubbed the chunk against it, and swirled the water with her hands.

Mrs. Kansteiner stood for a moment, hesitating for some reason I didn't know. Maybe she needed some time to think. She fiddled with the wet, soapy cloth in her hands. Her fingers rubbed between the shallow folds, as if searching for something in the gooey paste. In a moment, she nodded as if confirming the goodness of helping a new life come into Gonzales. Maybe she was wondering if I was grown enough to participate in such an event.

"Bring that wash water and come on in," she finally said.

I got the wash basin and followed her into the cabin.

We went into the sleeping room. There next to Mother on the big bed was a little pink baby, naked as they come. Mrs. Kansteiner wrapped the baby in the damp, soapy cloth and cleaned him up. In a short time she handed me my brother wrapped in a blanket Mama had recently crocheted. He was peaceful and curious, looking at me with new, glistening blue eyes. Our kindly neighbor continued to help Mama clean herself up and to lie on new bedding. When the job was completed, Mama took her infant son and settled into the bed.

When all was calm, Mrs. Kansteiner stood looking at Mama and the new baby. She touched the baby's head and said, "Rebecca,

I wish this child a peaceful and long life. I'll think of him in my Eugene's place."

Mama took her hand and the two women shared a long soulful look. Mama's lips formed the words, "Thank you."

Then Mrs. Kansteiner left us.

The days were long in September, and the men stayed in the fields until almost dark. As the sun was deep in the western sky, the silhouettes of two men and a tall, skinny boy appeared up the road. I ran out to meet them. When I told Daddy about his new son, he ran to the cabin.

My brother and I entered the sleeping room of our cabin. The scene that greeted us was the one I lived for. My adoring parents were captivated again by the wonder of their child. It was Daddy's first blood child, and Mama asked what he wanted to call the baby. Daddy thought for a long while, and then he said to call him Eugene. Mama smiled.

"Syd, come look at this." My brother had the old spelling book we so carefully packed and carried with us all the way from Kentucky. "Is this Eugene?" He pointed to a word in section four.

I looked at the page. "Yes, that's it. It means well-born." We looked at each other, wondering how the name could be so true. "He is well-born, John. It was just Mama and him, getting him born. They both did very well."

John nodded his head. He took the spelling book and studied it until the sunlight was gone.

My bewilderment of dirt and fear began to fade away that day. We had a secure home. The lye soap was sufficient. We had the love of family and the help of good friends. It was enough to get me through.

Early January 1832 – John Meets C.J, Ned, and Grace Dodson

By the time I was fifteen and my brother John was approaching thirteen, we were working like grown folks. Education was set aside. We knew from Susie's lessons in Kentucky how to read and write and calculate pluses and minuses, but those were not so important in Mexico. Physical strength, good health, and common sense were the greatest assets one could have as a young pioneer.

Gonzales was a blend of cultures brought there from a wide range of settler families. The white Americans who moved down from the United States brought their Irish, English, or German ways. People with white skin were called gringos. The word wasn't in our spelling book, but we were told it meant someone who was not easily understood in the Mexican culture.

There were blacks, too. Some free black folks claimed their own land. Other black folks came as servants in a gringo family, though it wasn't supposed to be legal. Others I suspected were from some cultural blend with traces of Indian blood like Mr. Chockow.

I was particularly intrigued with the Tejanos. They came out of the south, with the blood of old Spanish families. Tejas was really their land. They left the villages of southern Mexico and came into the frontier of northern Mexico for the same reasons we came. But they knew all the secrets. They knew the land, and they were generations ahead of the whites in conquering the environment.

There was a variety of languages spoken in the settlement. We had French speakers, Spanish speakers, and German speakers, all trying to communicate in pioneer English. We all wanted to blend ourselves to create a new local culture. We knew that could only be accomplished through intentional cooperation. The purpose of the community gatherings at the fire in the evenings was to blend ourselves together.

John advanced socially more quickly than I did. It was easy for him to start a conversation with a stranger. One night a boy named Ned Dodson befriended my brother.

"Hey, that's a swell cap you got. How'd you come by it?"

"My uncle gave it to me. He has a horse farm in Kentucky, and we rode for him. It was kinda a joke," John told him.

Ned's eyes grew big. "Naw, not in Kentucky! You mean it?"

"Sure enough," John said.

"Aw, we come from Kentucky. But we brought our horses with us, not just some red cap," Ned teased.

My brother was temporarily speechless. He took off his cap and slapped his leg, looking at me. I thought he would pop open with his excitement while he searched for his words. "Sydnie, did you hear that?" Then he turned to Ned and said, "Where is your farm? Where are the horses?"

"Out five miles from here. You walk that far, I'll show you!"

That conversation started my brother's new role in town. The Dodsons came from Kentucky several years ahead of us and were well-settled out on their place. The very next day, John walked out to see the Dodson farm. It was then John learned there were two Dodson children. Ned had a sister named Grace.

Grace Dodson was a freckle-faced tomboy. In spite of her rough and rugged ways, she was purely a natural beauty. She was plain-spoken, and she had opinions. Her body was lean and muscular. A crown of kinky brown curls hugged her head. The sun toasted her skin and bleached her eyebrows. She loved the horses, and she reminded John of home, back on Uncle Thomas's farm.

"She wears trousers," my brother said when he told me about her. "Trousers. And she rides. She looks like she just came in from Uncle Thomas's tracks!"

John's friendship with the Dodsons led to another good connection for him in town. My brother was smitten with the science of horses. Ned introduced him to the town's two blacksmiths.

One was Mr. Dickinson, and the other was a big German by the name of C.J. One evening, the two boys were laughing and carrying on. So I asked what it was all about.

"I'm gonna work for the blacksmiths, Syd. They asked me, and Daddy said I could."

"Yep, I knew ol' John would be a perfect hand for C.J.," Ned said. "Mr. Dickinson has been needin' help, because he has other responsibilities in town. Mr. C.J. works there, but with so many people coming here, they need more help. John is just what they need in that shop."

A blacksmith shop holds many a fascination for a young man. The livery was on St. Laurence Street, just a few blocks from our cabin. John loved being in there. He started with running errands and sweeping the floors. John learned quickly. C.J. began to train him in the ways of a blacksmith. In time he repaired broken tools and made new ones. John's compensation came in the form of eggs, bread, tortillas, and dried meats from C.J.'s Tejano wife. Our lives were soon enriched by John's new job.

This Mr. C.J. had a heavy German accent, and some other issues with talking clearly. He was difficult to understand, and he didn't like to talk. But John was fascinated with C.J.'s uniqueness. He saw working at the shop as an opportunity to meet folks, to do interesting things, and to learn German. John wanted so much to learn that he listened intently. He asked C.J. to teach him German, and in no time the two of them could hold a brief conversation in that language.

Then my brother began to pick up Spanish from the hands out on the Dodson farm. John Gaston had a gift for languages. In a year he was speaking English with the gringos, German in the shop with C.J., and Spanish with the Mexicans in town. He wasn't fluent, but he got by. This extra effort on John's part brought him more friends and made communication easier in the livery. C.J. didn't want to talk to anyone, and John could talk to everyone.

All this help allowed Mr. Dickinson to take care of other things in town, so it worked out just right.

Now, this blacksmith, C.J., was a living example of how things could go wrong, and how a beaten man could recover his dignity. He was well over six feet tall and stout. His round face bore the marks of violence. He was blind in his right eye and a jagged scar ran from the corner of that eye to his right ear. His one good eye protruded out strangely. John asked Ned about the scars, but the topic seemed bothersome to the Dodson boy.

"Oh, he got mad a while back cause some folks gave him grief about how he talks. It's nothin'. Just don't bring it up. He used to be a wild man, but not no more," Ned said.

John never again asked Ned about C.J.'s face. He didn't have to. We soon got information about the blacksmith without asking.

February 1, 1832 – John Finds Out C.J. Is a Schmidt Brother

My brother found great joy in his work, and he eagerly left our cabin early every morning to walk the few blocks over to the livery shop. He told us amusing stories, giving us a glimpse into his days there. Townspeople came in, and John learned more about the farmers—what they did and how they did it.

One evening the story was more personal. "Syd, come with me. We need to talk." I dried the supper dishes and told our parents we'd be back before dark. I assumed we'd go to the town square.

"What's eatin' you, little brother?" I started out the door.

"Come this way; we're going over toward St. Lawrence Street." We turned away from the town square. "Syd, I gotta tell you what happened today. I wasn't snoopin', I swear." He put both hands up facing me and shook his head.

"Okay, so you didn't snoop. What did you do?"

"I didn't do nothin'. I was just in there while C.J. took a big plow blade out to the Mueller place."

"That sounds innocent enough. Did you break something? Did you burn the place down?"

"No, Syd. Stop teasing me; I'm serious. I just was in there sortin' nails." He stopped in the middle of the street, slid his thumbs in his belt, and looked around, avoiding talk.

A woman passed our way carrying a sack of cornmeal, walking slowly with her little child. John tipped his red cap and gave her a "Howdy, ma'am."

Then in a quiet voice he said, "Let's go sit on the porch outside the shop. Nobody will think nothin' of us bein' there."

We walked along, just as casual as could be. Then we sat and he told me what happened.

"So, like I said, I was just in there mindin' the shop till C.J. came back. Then Mr. Miller came in. He had papers in his hand. He asked for C.J., and I told him he was gone; he'd be back later. So, Mr. Miller says to give C.J. these papers. I say, 'Sure thing,' and he holds 'em out so's I should take 'em. I took 'em, and I just looked at 'em, that's all, to see which way was up. I wanted to size 'em up and put 'em in a safe place." He stopped talking.

I waited while he gathered his thoughts. He looked at me like he expected a comment. I put out my hand, cocked my head, and waited for him to tell me more.

"Syd, have you ever really looked at C.J.?"

"Well, no. That would be rude. He's all scarred up, and it just wouldn't be polite to go lookin' at a man all marked up like that."

"But, Syd, I've been lookin' at him when we talk. That face, it's round and pudgy. And his one good eye, it sorta bugs out." John ran his hands around his own face.

"Okay, I guess you're right. So, why is all that so special?"

John pulled his knee up and turned sideways on the bench. He put his hands on the wood in front of him and leaned in to tell me clearly. "The papers were somethin' for business. There's a lot of boxes and lines drawn on the front. But bold as lightning, his full name was there." He squinted his eyes. "C.J.'s name is Schmidt. Carter J. Schmidt!"

I looked down at the brown wood and thought about it. *Is it possible? Could it be?*

"I really think he is Jeffrey Schmidt's baby brother, Carter."

I thought about that. Slowly I realized my brother made a convincing case. "Yes, I bet you're right. Are you going to ask him?"

"No, I'm just gonna wait. As time goes by, the truth will show itself. C.J. and his wife are good people. I want to know them for who they are now, not for who Carter might have been. I bet his wife doesn't know anything about his past." John turned back around, sat facing St. Lawrence Street and put his elbows on his thighs. "I don't want to make trouble for him. Mr. Dickinson respects him, and he deserves that. I just wanted to tell you, and I wonder if we should tell Daddy."

"Not yet. I think you can judge this thing for yourself. Even if he is the Schmidt brother, there's nothing to be done about it."

"Well, I think Mr. Jeffrey and Mr. Edgar would like to know their brother is alive and doing well," John said. "I'd like them to know he turned out good."

We sat for a few minutes, and I felt proud of my brother. In this place of violence and suffering, John was extending a private confidence in the goodness of his fellow man. He wanted to help heal a hurt and sponsor forgiveness. I liked that. I nodded at him. "John, you'll know when the time is right to tell Daddy. Come on, now. Let's go see who's down at the campfire," I said.

And we did.

February 2, 1832 – Sydnie Goes to Work at Mr. Miller's Place

My brother was really suited to this earthy new life in Tejas. His circle of friends enlarged quickly at the livery. One day he brought home a young man named Maclovio Guzman. The two met when Mac came in to the shop looking to buy some mules. Mac broke horses for the Dodsons, and he gave John practice talking in Spanish. He walked with a severe limp due to a horse falling on him some time back.

"They would have loved Mac back in Kentucky," John said. "The man knows horses." Mac struggled to walk, but he had more drive than four Kentuckians his age. The man was tall and imposing. He was known as Big Mac all over the territory. It turned out Mac was married to Anita, the energetic young woman who helped our mother at Mr. Miller's hotel on the first day we arrived. "I can learn a lot from Mac," John told me.

And I began to think about the value of a Tejano friendship.

Tom Miller came early to the DeWitt settlement. He was in Mexico back in 1822. Single men didn't get as much land as men with families, but Mr. Miller took what he was granted and made the most of it. He was a quiet, thoughtful man with no extravagances. His home was the smallest cabin in town, and he stayed focused on his business. Like the others, he came out here to make his future, and he didn't have much to say about his past.

With no other obligations, Tom Miller was able to invest all his efforts into the properties he had in town, and those investments were paying off. He built the two-story hotel on Water Street. On the bottom floor, he had a general store, a tavern, and the desk to register guests in the rooms upstairs. Those businesses were cornerstones of Gonzales's economy. Although he seldom drank, he sold a lot of corn liquor and had whatever other spirits he could get delivered to the tavern.

Nita kept everything going at the general store and the hotel during the day. When the sun went down and his work at the Dodson farm was finished for the day, Mac joined his wife, and the tavern opened for business. Tom depended on Mac for security. In spite of his limp, Mac could maintain order. Mac tended the tavern bar and generally kept the peace. Mr. Miller had good help, but it didn't seem enough.

Mr. Miller worked with a Mr. Kerr to mark boundaries, and he helped Mr. Green DeWitt coordinate documents for land titles from the Mexican government. During the first year we were in Gonzales, the town was growing fast. Business at Miller's Store was booming. All the leaders of town were busy with their responsibilities to the settlers, and Tom Miller was one of the leaders. Nita was struggling to keep up with all her work.

In January, Nita asked me if I wanted a job helping her at Tom's store. I was beginning to come out of my culture shock. By then, I had an idea that with work, Gonzales might someday be a place worth staying. I welcomed the chance to get out of our house and make a niche for myself in the town. Working in the store was a lot like what Mama and Susie did so well in our Kentucky inn. It seemed a perfect opportunity for me.

On the second day of February of 1832, I woke early. After waiting to get a cabin, surviving my fears from sounds of the night, evading the Indians, and living without sweet soap, I was growing up. I had a real job, and I'd get paid in real pesos. Finally, every member of the Davis family had a role in our town. We were fulfilling the second requirement on Mr. Jeffrey Schmidt's list. We would each contribute our bit to move the town ahead, not knowing how brief our time there would be.

March 11, 1832 – A Brief Marriage to Tom Miller

"What is he like, Nita?" I wanted to know about our boss, Mr. Miller.

"He's a loner," she said in her characteristic accent. "Never has a woman around him. He's a good man. We'll never be bothered. We just do our work and get to be together." Nita smiled with the joy of having a companion during the day before Mac came in the evening. She thought we'd have the place to ourselves, as Tom was preoccupied with his responsibilities to the town.

With Nita's description of his detachment, and the fact that Tom was old enough to be my father, it was rather unexpected when he immediately took notice of me. I thought at first maybe he just wanted to be sure I was a loyal employee and make sure I understood my chores. But in only a few days, I realized he was interested in more than my skill as a clerk in the general store. His eyes followed me, and then he began to find me alone.

I was inexperienced in the advances of men. Tom was my first beau. He was always attentive and generous to me. By early March, we were courting.

"You make Gonzales beautiful," he told me. "Life with you here will be better than I ever thought it could be."

In those days in the settlements of Tejas, there were many reasons to make a marriage match. There was admiration of sorts. Everyone wanted to feel safe, and many relationships were created for security. I suspect many marriages were contracts with very little emotion invested. For us, it was a comfortable fit into the community and the rhythm of life. Tom wanted a business partner, a life partner, and an heir. He was getting old and maybe lonely. Maybe he knew he was running out of time.

I can truly say there was love between us. Looking back, I can see it was a strange kind of love. There was a comfort that drew Nita, Mac, my brother John, Ned and his sister Grace, Tom, and me together. The time we spent together took me in the direction I needed to go, and I felt safe with Tom Miller. It all felt right, and our whirlwind courtship was encouraged by everyone in town. Of course, I talked to my mama about it, considering that Tom was much older than I was.

"Love is what matters, Sydna, love and care." We sat on the trot, and she reminded me how to use hindsight, even before things ever happen. "Close your eyes and imagine yourself married to Tom Miller," she said. "If you feel right, then we support your decision." Mama was always supportive.

I closed my eyes that night and imagined myself five years into the future. In my mind, Gonzales was thriving. Tom was an important man in town. We had a big house full of comfortable chairs on St. John Street. The windows were glass, edged with lace curtains. I imagined standing at my door talking to Nita, and we were both happy. I felt safe and clean. When I opened my eyes, I decided that's what I wanted.

Tom filed the appropriate papers. Preacher Stevenson was scheduled to be in Gonzales in March of 1832. We scheduled our marriage ceremony for then. The whole town was invited.

Nita helped me get a beautiful piece of brocade fabric from a trader going to Mexico City. Mama finished the dress just in time. She helped me put it on in an upstairs room in Tom's hotel. The tavern was packed. Daddy wore his black suit and walked me down the stairs to where Tom waited. The preacher said his words, and we replied with the appropriate responses.

My brother John brought in hams from the smoke house while Mac served drinks to everyone. Mama and Mrs. Kansteiner brought crocks of potato salad. The hotel smelled of Nita's fresh bread. Ladies from all around brought their best cakes and pies. Mama and Daddy danced to violin music. I felt like Gonzales royalty. It all felt right at the time.

Within a few months, I was expecting a child. Little Thomas arrived in February of 1833. I looked forward to my son playing with my little brother. But it didn't happen that way.

I knew lives could end. People died from cruelty, violence, or illness, but only after they experienced at least a few years of life. No one could have convinced me how quietly life could slip away from an innocent, well-loved new baby.

I wrapped him myself on his last night; warm from a fever. I laid him in the cradle next to our bed, only to find him blue and breathless the next morning. I lifted him from the cradle, realizing he had been too still, too quiet all morning. I tried to feel his breath. Not wanting to believe what I held, I tried to wrap his little fingers around my own, but they were cold and stiff. While I stood there in shock, Tom came to where we were. He took his son in his arms, not knowing. Then his face went white and he momentarily froze. Without a word he put his son back in my arms and walked out of the room. The child never took his first steps. We would never hear his first words. Whatever his personality would have been was forever known only to God.

My daddy took charge of the burial. Nita and Mac filled baskets with the early field flowers and fresh greenery to make a funeral parlor in the tavern. We received our friends there, in the same place we had been married. The tiny boy was wrapped in his own blanket, looking as sweet and peaceful as any living child. Someone had worked very hard to create a small coffin with flowers painted on the sides. Just as it had been on our wedding day, the whole town joined us. Two men picked up the tiny coffin and led a procession to the burial place on the edge of town.

Relationships under stress have their limitations. Perhaps Tom's purpose for our marriage was to be a father. Perhaps my purpose was to be Mrs. Somebody. Whatever our reasons, they dissolved with the death of our son.

Tom and I gradually found fewer things to discuss. We were still cordial and had our daily gatherings with our circle of friends at the tavern, but we didn't get along when we were alone. The hours I spent alone with Tom were my darkest, and he knew it. He avoided me.

One morning as he was eating breakfast in our little home, Tom very quietly asked me to sit down with him. I sat, and after a lot of quiet chewing he put his fork down, put his hands on his crossed knee, looked me calmly in the eye and said, "You need to be away from me now." Everything seemed very still.

I got up and poured two cups of coffee. "What do you have in mind?"

He laid out a very generous plan which indicated the depth of consideration this had taken. He would arrange a proper and legal separation and give me a room in the hotel. He said I could have a job in the tavern, and anything I needed for as long as I needed it.

I put my hand on his shoulder and looked out in the direction of the cemetery. "You're a good man, Tom Miller." I moved out of his house on St. John Street that very day and took a room at the hotel on Water Street. It seemed a good move. We both lived happier apart than when we lived together.

On the frontier, keeping a good relationship with someone you trusted gave a person a small measure of security, even if the relationship was strained. The reasons people spent time together might change, but folks were loyal in order to survive. Our marriage bond was legally dissolved in 1833. Because of our age difference, Tom became a father-figure to me. Nita and Mac still spent a lot of time with us. Supper in the tavern for Tom and Mac went on as usual. Nita continued to be my closest friend, and I continued to work in the store with her. Not much changed. Then something remarkable happened.

July 10, 1834 – Sydnie Meets John Benjamin Kellogg

Twenty-five cabins stood on lots in Gonzales by January of 1834. Late in February, lacy jade ferns began to unfurl around the edge of Mama's cabin on St. Louis Street. Soft gray-green leaves appeared on the tips of Daddy's pecan tree. I spent more time outside cracking open the fat brown nuts we collected the previous fall. In April, the fields were streaked with blue buffalo clover, joined by stalks of yellow yarrow in May. Nita showed me patches of berries on tangled vines, and we picked them in June. By July, the horizon sizzled in the hot stillness while grasshoppers danced. Evenings were blessed with the music of cicada wings, and harmony reigned over the promised land of Mexico.

More people moved to our town. Nothing of an urgent nature interrupted our lives for months. For pioneers creating a new town, a season of peace was exceptional. We had a piano in the tavern. Neighbors and friends gathered there in the evenings, which seemed like an improvement from the evening fires in the stone pit down by the new courthouse. On a good night, someone brought in a banjo or a guitar or sometimes a violin. The town buzzed with pleasure to be alive when the late summer sun went down in Gonzales.

At the end of one of these exceptional days, I was just going upstairs to my room when one of the talented musicians struck up a tune that got my attention. I stopped on the stairs to listen. The laughter in the room was inviting. Nita gave me one of her endearing, come-on-and-stay-a-while glances. My feet took me downstairs to the piano.

Glancing around the room, while pumping my knees to the beat of the music, I saw a tall, slender man with light curly hair standing in the doorway. I had seen him before, but I couldn't recall when or under what circumstances. It was that unanswered question that wouldn't let me look elsewhere.

He walked over to Mac, asked for some food, and sat down with a glass of whiskey in his hand. He took a sip of his whiskey, swished the liquid around in his mouth, and drew it over his teeth to savor the flavor. A partial smack pulled at the corner of his mouth. He sat the glass on the table, gave it a nod, leaned forward in his chair, and began to eat his supper. He leaned back in his chair and chewed. Then he looked up from his plate. His eyes looked straight at me, and he smiled. For the life of me, I couldn't recall where, but I knew we had met before. I felt conspicuous and tried not to stare. Then I realized he was still watching me.

John Benjamin Kellogg Jr. had come to eat, drink, and mingle. Having gotten his food and drink, he was ready to socialize. He finished eating and approached a small gathering of my friends. He struck up a conversation with a man I knew. The man introduced us, and Johnny Kellogg asked me to dance.

As we swirled, he began to talk. "You remember back in January I come to talk to Tom about my daddy's farm papers?" he reminded me.

Finally I did remember. "Well, yes I do remember now. Your family just got here last winter."

"Yep. We just been here a while." We finished the dance.

He pulled out a chair for me and we sat down.

"My paw was givin' me a piece of ground, and I needed Tom to separate it out on the papers."

"Oh, I understand." I adjusted my skirt.

"I'm buildin' me a cabin now." He sat back in the chair looking proud.

"And I bet it'll be a good one." I was searching for things to say.

"I saw you that day, working in the store. I asked about you over at the livery. Turns out it was your brother I asked!"

"Yes, this is a small town, and that was my brother."

"Well, he told me you were Tom's wife. Man, I thought Tom was mighty lucky to have such a pretty young wife," Johnny confessed. After a pause, he brought it up as a question. "But you're not married no more? You know how things get talked about in town."

Everyone in Gonzales knew our business, and John Kellogg had heard the gossip. Everyone knew about our dead baby and our divorce arrangement.

I was a bit embarrassed, but I wouldn't let the chance to explain slip away. "Oh, that was just something we were going through," I said. "Making a way out here, being friends, getting married; those are things that take a lot of understanding, more understanding than we knew back then."

Music started, and we stood up to dance again. I could barely breathe, looking into his hazel eyes. The strength in his arms wrapped around me was like steel, and I felt as if I was dancing on air.

"I know," he agreed. "You're right," he continued in a slow, thoughtful way. "It's a tough life out here. Person gotta really work at life if we gonna make it." He twirled me around. "But..." he drew out his words thoughtfully as we made a few turns around the floor, "a pretty young gal like you might do fine with a younger man...like me, for instance." He looked down into my eyes with an expression serious as a preacher.

I studied his face. The music was over too soon.

He led me over to the table, and we sat down. He pushed his empty plate aside and spoke sincerely. "I'm really sorry about all you went through. Life is hard enough out here without you losing a little baby and all that. Me and Tom been friends since I come out here. I know he's a good man. He just wasn't right for you."

I was nervous about these topics and about the feelings I was having about this man. The memories were sad, but talking to John

Kellogg about them gave me a new perspective. I felt my loss filling up with hope.

Realizing my discomfort with the conversation, he changed the direction of it. He pulled out a remarkably clean handkerchief and wiped his brow. "Can I get you somethin'?"

I declined, feeling dangerously interested in him.

"I tell you what, Miss Sydnie. You just smile your pretty smile and enjoy this evenin'. I'm real glad you came back down those stairs." He looked toward the piano and nodded his head in time with the music.

We sat together for two more songs while Johnny slowly emptied his second whiskey glass. Then he winked at me. "Wanna dance again?" He took my hand and swirled me up on the floor.

We danced and laughed. I was transformed with the pleasure I found in his company. As the night wore on, I became truly happy for the first time since Kentucky.

We were the last to leave. The night had flown by. Mac and Nita were sweeping up and making their jobs last longer than they had to when I realized the tavern was empty. Johnny walked me to the foot of the stairs, knowing I would go up to my room from there. He put an arm on either side of me and held onto the stair rail.

"Miss Sydnie, I think you need a little fun in your life," he said.

I couldn't think of a reply, but he didn't rush me.

He quietly said, "I'm gonna go now. But I'll be back. Until then, I want you to think about how life might be out here if you were to be with a younger man, a man who could show you some fun like we had tonight."

He dropped his arms from the rail. As his hands came down, mine moved up, and our fingers intertwined. I didn't know what to say, so I just giggled. All I could do was look at him.

"I made you laugh," he said. "Will you think about it?"

I nodded, and he winked again. He backed away and went out the door, smiling all the way.

Prairie folks had a matter-of-fact way of conducting business. After our divorce, whatever Tom thought or felt about me was demonstrated as fatherly concern. He was supportive in everything I did. Tom considered the Kellogg family his friends, and that didn't change. John Benjamin Kellogg and I courted for the next full year. John made it his business to know without a doubt that Tom was in the past, and that I could recommit to another marriage. We talked. We agreed. I could commit.

The next spring we filed our intention to live as husband and wife. Tom Miller filed our papers. In June of 1835, I moved my things to John Kellogg's little cabin out on the Kellogg place. I stopped working in the tavern except when Nita needed extra help. Life with John Kellogg was fun as we began to inch our way into the future as a couple. The bond among the young pioneers in Gonzales continued to strengthen for the months we had left before history claimed our legacy.

Part 3:

The Land of Broken Promises

August 1, 1835 – Politics Enter the Family Concerns

Putting my previous failures behind me, I was ready to be a wife again. John Benjamin had his own cabin, which became our home. It was a one-room structure facing south, about a half mile from town. We had two window openings and a front door. Deerskin flaps were tacked over each window. The roof was a flat plane sloping down toward the north.

A single shelf ran across the north wall from corner to corner. Nita gave me a bolt of eyelet lace. I fastened it to the shelf letting the lace peek just a smidge over the front edge. Mother gave me four blue-and-white-speckled glazed plates and four matching cups that sat upon the shelf. Under the shelf was a long wooden storage trunk attached to the wall. The trunk, which had two hinged lids, served as our bench. A split log with three legs served as a table in front of the trunk. A small wood stove sat near the west wall.

Along the east wall, our pallet was unrolled each night and rolled up each morning. Out back in the little barn, all John Benjamin's tools were neatly hung on the walls. He built a one-horse stall to protect his horse at night. Two hens and a red rooster scratched in our yard. Farther away from the cabin was a privy. We had everything a family needed.

A rain barrel with a tin drinking dipper was standing just outside the door at a convenient distance. I bought a broom at the general store and used it every day. Mama let me bring vegetables from her garden. We kept them in a wooden bowl on the three-legged table. The cabin was orderly every day. I made sure of that, because my husband liked order.

The smell of my corn biscuits and beans lured my husband back to our front door every day about noon. He came in from the fields and teased me till he finished eating. Then he went back out to tend the corn and peas. We had our routine. But while we might maintain a predictably ordinary life within our cabin, the world outside our home was slipping into chaos.

Using the decoy of land grants, Mexico had invited folks to settle there because she needed farmers to anchor the culture in her massive northern ranges, to help control the Indians, and eventually to pay taxes. That invitation was offered back in the early 1820s. We came, and we expected our rewards, including proper titles to our land, citizenship, and governmental protections. But it wasn't happening that way. Too many people had come. Mexico was unable to provide what she promised. We had word that a new leader had taken control, and we were no longer wanted. Antonio López de Santa Anna had been elected President of Mexico. His greatest fear was that the United States would annex Tejas. After all, by 1835 Tejas was full of gringos from the United States.

Stephen Austin and Green DeWitt contracted with Mexico to settle hundreds of immigrants, but they couldn't obtain proper papers. In January of 1835, Austin went to Mexico City to appeal for those contracts to be honored with legal documents. Austin was charged with treason and thrown in jail. After we got word of Austin's arrest, Mr. DeWitt went down there to see if he could inspire some help. His efforts were rewarded with a case of cholera, and Mr. DeWitt died in May.

Gonzales folks were feeling anxious. Ad hoc meetings were conducted in the tavern to discuss our concerns, and all the Davises and the Kelloggs attended. Tom Miller called on my daddy to give his opinions.

"George, you've got law training. What rights do we have here? How do you see this thing? What are we gonna do to get our proper documents?"

Being a humble man, Daddy shook his head as if to take a pass. "I don't know. This here is Mexico. Our US laws don't apply. They used the US constitution for their first model. But now, with this Santa Anna, I just don't know. He's a different kind of a man."

Another man stood. "Over in Mina they took control of ther'selves already. They done formed up a local committee in town to make their own decisions; they gonna make their own laws. Why can't we do that? We get more help from each other than we ever get from the Mexican government."

Tom looked at Daddy.

After some thought, Daddy said slowly, "We could do that. We can form a local committee to study this, and they can collect information. Then a report can be brought back to the town for a discussion."

A low rumble of deep voices began and grew into a throng of confusion. Tom rapped the handle of a knife on the tavern bar. All went quiet.

"Davis, will you head up such a committee?"

Daddy nodded his head and stood up. "This here is new ground we're facin'. I'll do it if six others will join me."

"I'll sign up with you, Davis."

"Put me down for that, Tom."

Commitments came from all over the room. It was settled. We'd have a local committee.

As the gringos from the Unites States were celebrating the decision, I saw two Tejanos with sober expressions leave the tavern. They mounted their horses and headed down the San Antonio road out of town. Austin's appeal for his settlers' documents had been viewed by Santa Anna as treason. I wondered if the men of Gonzales were now guilty of the same crime.

In the early months of my marriage to John Benjamin, we began to be concerned with spies and betrayal. When I heard hushed voices sharing gossip from Mexico, I thought of one man. That was Juan Seguin. He was a regular guest at the tavern, and now he was also a regular visitor in the Davis home. Nita had shown great respect for him. She told me he was venerated among the Tejano population. His well-connected family had great influence with the Mexican government.

Mr. Seguin sat with Daddy out on the trot regularly. When I studied him closely, there was no mistaking his intelligence. He could be sly. Seguin was a wiry, dark Tejano who could charm the scales off a rattlesnake. Sometimes he disguised himself to get information. It was Señor Seguin who informed the town of Austin's arrest and imprisonment. He was a guest in my parents' home the night my father called us all together and told us, "You young folks need to watch your mouth. Keep your ideas to yourself. We'll work this out in time, but you stay out of it for now," he advised.

Like most folks, we kept our ideas to ourselves and simply conducted the work of the day. But the spies got word to Mexico City of a potential revolt. Santa Anna was not pleased. Fear and suspicion were festering. Very little was being admitted out loud by the gringos. But by summer of 1835, the notion of rebellion was spreading quietly underground like the roots of the prairie grass.

August 1835 – News of a Kellogg Baby

In spite of the political confusion overtaking Gonzales by late summer, our lives in the Kellogg cabin were taking shape. Life took on a pattern, and there was a rhythm in our home. My days were scheduled for the washing, for helping Nita, for paying a visit to Mama, and all those things married ladies were expected to do. The world seemed calm for a season.

Daddy D. was working with Mr. Nash from Old Scotts. They made a plan for people in Gonzales to send letters back to family in the states. The town folks were told they could submit letters and Mr. Nash would take them to Matagorda. Then a trusted man would take them to Mr. Edgar Schmidt in New Orleans, who would pass them on to his brother. Mr. Jeffrey Schmidt would do all he could to deliver them to the intended persons.

Mama wrote about Eugene and addressed her letter to Susie Gaston-Morgan in Green River, Kentucky. Daddy collected the letters and tied them in a bundle. Mr. Nash took them to the Bay, and off they went on a boat headed for New Orleans.

In that peaceful season I had time to daydream, enjoy nature, and imagine the life I wanted. I collected some fern shoots and wild verbena from Mama's garden and planted them along the front of my house, remembering how Jonas had done it in Kentucky. John Benjamin brought stones and we set them in the ground to pave a welcome path leading to our front door. It wasn't the Green River Inn, but the place took on a distinctive appearance. I wanted folks to feel drawn to our place. I put in a little vegetable garden of my own, drawing on the precious memories of my childhood.

John Benjamin left for the cornfields just after breakfast, came back for lunch, and then worked till sundown. Awakening in the morning was a happy time in our little cabin. Even the morning sickness that started in July gave me joy because I knew what it meant. In late August when I was sure, I confided to my husband that we were going to be parents. I told him in the morning, just as he was leaving. He reacted with apprehension.

He stood in the open doorway for a while, leaning with one hand against the door frame. Then he turned, closed the door and came back to me. He put a trembling hand gently on of each of my shoulders. With a quivering lip he asked, "You gonna be okay, Syd?"

"Sure. This one will make it," I told him. "This one will make it, and this one will make our family proud," I assured him.

He wrapped me in his arms, and we cried. Then we pulled ourselves and our resilience together and pledged our devotion. He went to find my brother. Within twenty-four hours, the whole town knew our happy news.

With a child coming, home and family doubled in importance. I hoped that life would finally settle into what I had envisioned before we left Kentucky. But little did I know, life would not be settling down for anybody in Gonzales in 1835.

September 1835 – John Gaston Spies; Daddy Buries the Cannon Under a Peach Tree

In the last week of September, the days were growing shorter and the heat was letting up. The rain kept us inside our cabins that year. On a particularly gray morning, I was hanging some wash inside the house when I heard my brother ride up. He reined in his horse, swung his leg over the bare back, and slid off.

"What are you doing, little brother?" I asked.

"Where is John Benjamin? I need to talk to him."

"He left for the fields early this morning and won't be back till noon. Can I tell him something for you?"

My brother had a serious look. He pulled off that faded red cap and slapped the leg he had propped on my front stoop. "Syd …." His voice was quiet. He glanced to the woods and back. He leaned against the front of our cabin and took a deep breath that slowed his words. He pulled at the seam that held his sleeve to his shirt and ran the fabric across beads of sweat along the skin under his nose. A tender crop of dark whiskers tried to make a mustache above his upper lip. I thought about how grown he was, and I admired his role in town as a respected young man. I thought how much help he was to Mama. What he had to say was important to him. I looked at him with serious expectation.

"I'm going to the river to listen to the Mexicans, Syd."

"What Mexicans?"

"Shhh." He motioned with his hands to lower my voice. "There's soldados on the other side of the river." He gestured toward the Guadalupe. "Two of Seguin's men came in last night to tell us. They watched them all day. We think they want that cannon. If they knew how broke it is, they wouldn't bother, but they brought an empty cart to take it back. The river is too high for them to cross just yet. Tom asked me and Mac to go listen and see what we can find out. We'll be back tomorrow. You tell John Benjamin when he gets home. Will you do that, Syd?"

"Sure, John, of course I'll tell him about it. You just take care of yourself."

For a few seconds we looked at each other, wondering what might result from this mission. He grinned at me and led the horse next to our stoop. He flung his leg over and was off at a trot. As he rode away, I imagined my brother sitting quietly in the woods, remembering the day we saw the Indian boy with the dog. John Gaston was grown now, helping support our mother. He understood Spanish and would use that to protect our town. A shudder ran down my back.

In the middle of our town, a newly constructed courthouse sat in the center of a freshly swept courtyard. Along the stone walk, in front of a graceful mesquite tree sat a humble cannon. It had been there for a few years, providing us a sense of security. The Mexican government loaned it to Gonzales to prove their partnership in our efforts against Indian raids on the town. Now, after years of displaying the cannon in the center of town, Gonzales was expected to give it back.

There were spies among us. Someone got to Mexico City with information about our local committee, and Santa Anna suspected a rebellion. He wasn't going to help us with that. The evidence of someone's betrayal was now camped in the woods, planning in

Spanish how to deny us what little protection we had. My own little brother was going to help stop them.

There was no particular reason for my brother to tell my husband about his night on the river listening to a Spanish conversation. But this had become their way. My brother adored John Benjamin, and my husband cherished their bond. Sharing their work was as important as doing it. That night I told my husband about my brother's assignment, and he had concerns for me.

"You go to your mother's in the morning," Johnny instructed. "I don't want you out here alone. We need to find out what's going on."

As I often had, I felt safety in his protection, and I loved it. I'd do whatever he said was best. The very next morning I was at my Mama's cabin early.

When I arrived, I stopped by the door to Mama's cooking room to scrape the mud from my shoes. I noticed Daddy's boots sitting there, packed with fresh mud. He had already been outside, even before dawn. My parents were sitting inside drinking coffee by the light of an oil lamp. Daddy's feet were bare, but his clothes were wet and muddy. I could tell he had already been outside working, but it was barely light.

"What are you doing out so early this morning?"

"Never you mind, girl," Daddy said, teasing me with a smile. "Come in here and get some coffee."

It wasn't Christmas or anyone's birthday, but I sensed secrecy—the kind you know better than to ask about. As soon as I poured my coffee, my daddy said he needed to go to a meeting at the tavern, and he left.

"Mama, what is Daddy doing?" I could barely make out his silhouette as he pulled his boots on outside, but I noticed he went to the back of the house, not toward a meeting in town.

Mama pretended not to hear, and she changed the subject. "Your brother was out all last night, Sydna. I'm looking for him to come in." She took Daddy's tin cup and put it in the big wash basin. She stood by the stove, and after a thoughtful pause, she tried to explain. "Sydna, things are looking a bit dangerous. George is working with the men in town to keep the violence down. Sometimes it's better if you don't know everything. Just trust that we're all goin' to get through this together." She patted my hand and tossed her cold coffee into the wash basin.

Eugene came through the door rubbing his eyes. I knew his favorite place was out on the trot, and I wouldn't miss a chance to take him out there. We went outside, where I heard noises coming from around the back of the house. I waited. In a very few seconds, my daddy and two other men came around, and I realized the secret. They were pushing the little cannon on its cart. It was covered with mud, squeaking and groaning as the men rolled it in the direction of Water Street.

When Daddy and the men were well away from our cabin, I bundled my little brother in my arms. "Let's go to the garden, Eugene." Light was just beginning to break at the tree line. In the gray of the morning, I could tell the cannon had been buried overnight under one of Daddy's peach trees. The poor thing leaned at an awkward angle. The men had unearthed the cannon in the dark. Their efforts to replant the tree were insufficient.

With darkness still concealing them, John Gaston and Mac Guzman returned in the very early morning to give their report to a small contingent of men sitting at a corner table in Tom Miller's tavern. My brother described the scene to us when he came back home later that morning.

"We told the committee there's five, maybe six uniformed soldiers camped down on the river. They want the cannon, but they need help crossing the river." My brother laughed and poked at me. "Daddy buried that cannon last night, so's they couldn't come get it."

Mama shot me a look of concern and turned away.

"Mac was telling Tom this morning when one of the soldados came into the tavern. Using a lot of hand gestures, he held out a note, and Tom read it to us. They said they want the cannon back. And they said it's our duty to return it. That's when I left. I need a bite of biscuit, then I need to get back over there."

"You need a good night's sleep," Mama told him.

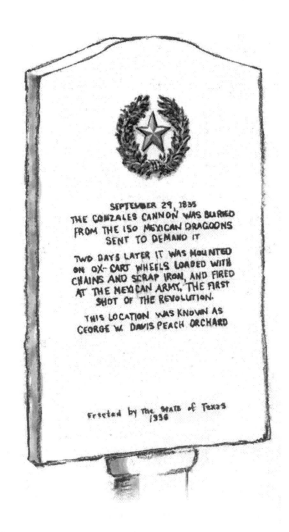

SEPTEMBER 29, 1835
THE GONZALES CANNON WAS BURIED
FROM THE 150 MEXICAN DRAGOONS
SENT TO DEMAND IT

TWO DAYS LATER IT WAS MOUNTED
ON OX-CART WHEELS LOADED WITH
CHAINS AND SCRAP IRON, AND FIRED
AT THE MEXICAN ARMY, THE FIRST
SHOT OF THE REVOLUTION.

THIS LOCATION WAS KNOWN AS
GEORGE W. DAVIS PEACH ORCHARD

Erected by The State of Texas
1936

Cannon Burial Place

"No, Ma, I gotta see what's gonna happen now." He looked at me. "Where's John Benjamin?"

I just looked at him and shrugged, not really knowing where my husband was with all the confusion in town.

John stuffed a biscuit in his shirt pocket and stopped by the well pump to wash his face. Mac found him there and told us what was happening back at the tavern. "They're trying to bluff. They're pretending concern for returning the cannon, but they're really just stalling. John Benjamin came, and he's looking for you over there."

My brother went with his friend back to the tavern.

"The ferry is broken. You'll have to wait. It might be ready tomorrow." Tom Miller was talking to the soldier, who hesitated and looked at Tom as if translating each word into his language.

When John and Mac arrived, they relayed the message in Spanish. The Mexican soldier finally understood.

"Gracias, Señor," he replied. He executed a half-hearted salute, bowed slightly, and clicked his heels.

The Mexican headed for the door leading outside of the tavern. Before he could make his exit, another man from Gonzales came in, and he handed the soldier a note signed by the highest city official.

The note read,

> I am removed from Gonzales on a mission to visit with my superiors, after which I will know the best procedures. If I learn we are required to relinquish the field piece, we will do so immediately. Further, we are reduced in numbers of men to help with this endeavor, and we trust you will accept what little assistance we can offer. We remain in your debt.
> Signed, Andrew Ponton
> Alcalde of Gonzales

Mr. Ponton did not lie. There were very few men in Gonzales when the note was written, because they had all ridden away from town to get help. Within hours the situation would be reversed, as help was already on its way. By the time the Mexican soldiers would come for the cannon, they would be outnumbered.

Frontiersmen by this time knew to make sly use of whatever resources came their way. Gonzales men used the bad weather and politics to buy twenty-four hours of precious time.

October 1, 1835 – The Come and Take It Flag

On the first day of October, a Mexican Army lieutenant grew impatient as he sat in his camp along the Guadalupe River. He sent a messenger across the river to Gonzales, asking to speak with the Alcalde. But the men of Gonzales stalled for time again. Andrew Ponton had no intention of discussing the cannon. The Mexicans were told that bad weather prevented Ponton's return. He would come find them as soon as he arrived.

While the Mexicans waited, they moved to the high ground some distance from the flooding river. They made camp in Ezekiel Williams's farm field.

Pop Kellogg came in the house and told us more than one hundred recruits from Columbus, Moore's Fort, and other communities just slipped into town. Most left their horses out at the Dodson's so they could walk in without notice. All those volunteers were hiding out on the river bank, waiting for a confrontation.

Everything was set. The Mexicans still believed Gonzales was short of men and thought they would overpower us.

While Pop Kellogg and Mama were drinking the last of their coffee, Georgia Samuels stepped into Mama's front door. "Rebecca, you and Sydnie come on over to the DeWitt place. Gather up your sewing notions and come on. John Senior, you go see if Elizabeth wants to come, too. We're fixin' to send Santa Anna a message from us women." She left with a "Harrrumph!"

"Come on, Syd, let's go see," Mama said. Sarah DeWitt was a widow now, but she was as determined as her husband had been to see Gonzales succeed.

I handed Mama my sewing basket and took Eugene by the hand. We went to the DeWitt cabin and joined a covey of women. There on the table was a section of beautiful white linen approximately three feet by four feet cut from the skirt of Naomi DeWitt's precious wedding dress. The DeWitts were putting all they had into this campaign. Jane Marsh brought a pair of black trousers her son had outgrown. From one leg of the trousers the women fashioned the shape of a cannon barrel. I dug into the sewing basket and brought out two spools of heavy, black mending thread. Needles were distributed and soon a convincing black cannon appeared on the white field of cloth. Then brilliance struck.

Our defiance would be clearly communicated in large letters embroidered under the cannon. The inspired women worked together and in no time a banner was ready. By early evening the message was complete. The words COME AND TAKE IT were embroidered in black. It was a dare to the soldados who intended to take our property.

Jane Marsh took the banner to the blacksmith shop where the cannon was being reworked. They cut a stiff branch and attached the banner. Later that evening, the little cannon was taken to the woods with the flag flying over it.

Mama and I took Eugene back to St. Louis Street and spent the night listening for sounds of the next confrontation. John

Come and Take It Flag

Gaston, Daddy, and John Benjamin all went out toward the river. The night was very quiet. Not even the crickets sang.

October 2, 1835 – Confrontation in the Farm Field (Battle of Gonzales)

October second dawned foggy. I went to the hotel to find Nita. We crawled up to the attic of the hotel and looked out the slats in the attic vents. That was the highest point of town, and we could see beyond Water Street, across the river, and into the Williams's farm field. Soldiers in gray pants sauntered in casual rows. Two men dressed in blue pants with tall hats rode on horses around the rows of men.

Opposite the formation in the field and back in the woods along the river, we knew were Big Mac, John Benjamin, and all the rest. We strained to see in that direction to catch a glimpse of them. After some time, the volunteers began to appear, one by one, then many at the same time. With their long rifles across their arms, they walked boldly out into the open in small groups. Then several men rolled out the cannon. A breeze caught the banner from the bottom. The white fabric unfurled elegantly to display the words COME AND TAKE IT, and my heart pounded with the excitement.

The Mexican officer turned his horse in the direction of the river. He must have realized they were outnumbered, and he couldn't have missed the flag. Suddenly he reined his horse up short and galloped around to the front of the formation. The officers pointed and gestured to the soldiers on the ground. The men in gray pants took up their arms and stood at attention in straight rows.

One man on a horse drew a long sword and held it over his head as the horse circled. Unintelligible voices were heard, and the front row of soldiers went to their knees. The man on the horse pointed the sword toward the river and yelled, "Fire!"

I froze for a moment, searching to see who I might recognize in the front line of volunteers. Sparks flared out and smoke drifted up from the barrels of the Mexican rifles. Then we heard the percussion of the volleys. But the distance was too great. The bullets never reached our men.

In short order, the Gonzales men blew out a blast of the little cannon. Kaboom! It had been loaded with chain and scrap metal and was fully capable of expressing our sentiments. Those shots must have reached the front ranks, as one soldier fell back on the ground. Several men near the fallen soldier picked him up by his legs and arms and carried him away. The rest stood up and ran for the woods behind Williams's field. Then all was quiet. I stood with Nita, holding my breath.

Time passed. My heart was pounding with concern. A man from the Mexican side rode out from the protection of the trees. He held his rifle above his head. He was dressed as a farmer, not in a uniform. He had no sword. He sat on his horse, alone in the center of the field for some time, facing the river. Then one of the men with a sword and uniform joined him. Those two men brought their horses side-by-side and waited.

Suddenly someone from the Gonzales group trotted his horse out from the river and galloped up to the two men waiting out there. They appeared to be talking. The conversation must have become more intense because the Gonzales rider suddenly turned his horse back toward the river. The horse took a dead run and the rider shouted, "Fire." As bullets came from the river, the two remaining riders fled to the woods. The Mexicans left. The cannon came back to Gonzales.

There was a spirit of victory in Gonzales then, with only a shallow tinge of caution. The men were emboldened. A shot from the noise-maker cannon was not much more than a threat. She was symbolic of our determination. Her real value was in our refusal to give it up.

Defending the cannon in Gonzales was a turning point for all the families Austin and DeWitt brought into Mexico. What started as a conversation about broken promises turned into a movement for independence. Many good men would die before the movement was complete.

Mid-October 1835 – The Lancers Go to San Antonio

In the deep fall of 1835, I walked to my mama's cabin on St. Louis Street to harvest the bounty of nuts from Daddy's pecan tree. The woods whistled with a cold wind that sounded like a warning. I wondered as I walked to town, *What will the news be today?* The Tavern hosted informants every night. They were spies bringing reports of Mexican troops discovered in the woods from the Guadalupe all the way to the Gulf coast. The Mexicans could smell the insubordination carried by men dedicated to Texian justice.

We heard the stories. Back as early as May, we heard about the sacking of the city of Zacatecas. Two-thousand civilians—not one in uniform, just common farmers, their children and wives—had been ravaged with the worst kind of Mexican debauchery. It was a raid inspired by rumors of rebellion. The Mexican Army matched the Comanche that day with their wickedness in Zacatecas. And in September, even closer to home, some Mexicans broke into a storeroom and beat in the brains of the farmer boy they found in there.

Our hearts went out to the victims, and we shuddered alongside our neighbors. We knew every community was prey to Indians or raiders of any persuasion. But so far, Gonzales restrained from retaliation. We wanted to believe these assaults were exceptions, carried out by renegade scouts acting on their own. The battle for our cannon was our personal fight. I secretly hoped the rest of the stories would continue to be about other places. Gonzales had enough trouble at home that year. We left other folks' business to other folks.

Stephen Austin, a highly respected man, was now out of his Mexican jail cell. He had been a good friend of the deceased Mr. DeWitt. They had a history together, including being partners in this notion of settling Tejas. Austin knew the land. He knew the Mexican leaders, and he knew the Mexican law. He also knew that without DeWitt, Gonzales needed him. The settlers drafted Austin to organize an effort to control all the threats. Loose as it was, a rebel force was forming with no real obligation other than their sense of loyalty.

One night late in October, Mr. Seguin came in the tavern. "They come into San Antonio by the hundreds!" he said. "They keep a whole arsenal in their headquarters, that ol' Spanish mission near the town square."

That night the news stirred more reaction. The Gonzales men, under the influence of either corn liquor or their own bravado, decided to form a fighting unit.

John Benjamin was in the tavern that night. When he came home, he said, "Sydnie, I need your broom." I knew he was a bit tipsy, but I gave him the broom. He propped it by the front door, muttered a few words, and we went to bed. I never suspected what he planned.

The next morning instead of going to the field, he went to his barn and sharpened a file. He removed the broom straw, put a long notch in the broomstick and fitted the file in as if it was a blade. In a short while he was stooped over at the well pump wetting a length of leather strapping. He pulled the strapping tight, wrapped it around the joint and tucked the tail into the last loop.

"That'll tighten up when she dries," he said, satisfied with himself.

"What are you doing?" I wanted to know.

"Sydna, I'll get you another broom." He sheepishly held out the straw from the sweeping end of my broom. Then he turned the long wooden pole in his hands and stabbed it out into the air. "Austin is gonna need us, and we're gonna go. We're gonna be the Gonzales Lancers," he said.

I just laughed, but he looked at me, all serious.

"Come with me to town. You can visit with your mama, and we'll see how this goes over."

I had to go, just to know what he was up to.

John Benjamin carried his broomstick upright, the blade pointed skyward. I was quiet as we walked, remembering the day my brother and I evaded the Indian boy fishing with his spear and his dog and the skunk at the river. I wondered if my husband was having a game with his drinking buddies or if this lance had a more serious meaning.

"What you thinking about, girl?" He smiled and shot a look down at me.

For a precious moment we were courting again, just walking in the cool October air without a care.

"I'm just wondering what they're going to say when you come into town with that broom stick."

"Well, Missy, you weren't there last night. You don't know about the Lancers." He grinned and broke into a run.

We were already crossing St. Andrews Street, and then we followed St. Joseph Street toward the other side of town. Much to my surprise, the men we met along the way hailed him.

"Hey, Lancer, that looks fine!"

"See? I told you," he said smugly. He let me catch up to him.

We turned on St. Lawrence Street so John Benjamin could go to the livery. I went on to the store on Water Street.

"I don't know what it's about," I told Nita.

"I tell you," she said. "Last night they all feel like they got to fight."

Then she told me how one man got up on the bar with her broom and told the men to go home, get their wives' brooms, and make a lance like my husband did. They planned to form a unit and call themselves the Gonzales Lancers. They wanted to be ready so when Austin needed them, they'd be more organized. It was serious business. I went to my mama's cabin.

At noon, my brother and my husband joined us in Mama's cabin. "Everyone in the county wants a file sharpened." My brother poured himself a cup of coffee. "This Lance Brigade is the thing," he said as he grabbed a biscuit and propped a foot behind him against the wall.

"We gotta go," John Benjamin told me. The reason for his urgency to leave became clear as soon as we stepped out onto the trot of Mama's cabin. "We gonna go to San Antone," he said. "All the Lancers." He was walking briskly, as if something was left on the fire.

I was having trouble keeping up with him. "Why? Why now?"

"Because, we gotta cut this off now. The Mexicans are buildin' up a force. We tried to make a point with the cannon, but they are still determined to give us grief." He stopped in the middle of the street. "You heard what they did in Zacatecas. Word is Santa Anna's Army is taking over every village. If they take San Antone, we'll be helpless. The Tejanos don't want that. Nobody around here wants a dictatorship." He stood looking at me. Then he started walking again, each step of his boots pounding the earth. "Austin sent word he's coming through here. We gonna be ready to go with him and cut this off now."

They all met the next day down in the town square. It seemed like a snake hunt to me. No real reason, just looking for trouble to flex some muscle and air some grievances. I wondered if it would make any difference—get anybody's farm papers or stop the Indians from burning down barns and scalping.

October was a dormant season in between crops. The work in the fields was not so demanding. If they had to go find trouble, this was the best time of the year to get it off their collective chests. In my third month of expectancy, I really didn't want my husband going down to San Antonio, but I figured better to go and get back, so he'd be there in the spring for the baby.

The next two weeks were dedicated to the planning and drawing out of folks wanting to join the Gonzales Lance Brigade. I kept hoping the glamour would wear thin and they would change their minds. But they didn't.

Austin really did come through Gonzales with about a hundred men. Mr. Austin and his officers stayed in the hotel. The volunteers camped all over creation. They left town the last week of October. The Gonzales men were all holding a lance, and the little cannon was riding on a new cart with oversized wheels. The COME AND TAKE IT flag proudly waved from a pole on the cannon cart. It was a sight to remember. Nobody thought they'd be gone very long.

December 13, 1835 – John Benjamin Reflects on San Antonio (The Battle for Bexar)

More than a month later, in December, I was trying to break the ice that had formed in the rain barrel. I noticed two riders coming up the road from Gonzales. One animal looked like John Benjamin's horse, so I took more notice. With a closer look, I could identify my husband, so I ran out to meet them. They were traveling slow. John Benjamin hobbled into the cabin with the help of his friend, Trapper Cain.

"What happened?" I asked.

"It's really nothing but a sprain," John said.

Trapper sorted out their gear and went on his way. John Benjamin was struggling to walk, so he lay on the bench against the wall.

"I'll pull out the bedroll," I offered.

He discouraged it. "No, just sit here with me." He held my hand and tugged gently on my arm, tapping on the bench where he wanted me to sit.

He hugged me to him, and I could smell his skin again. It was like the warm earth in spring, giving a promise of good things to come.

"Okay." I squeezed into the space where he tapped. I kissed his face all over, and he smiled at me. "Tell me what happened," I asked, and he began to tell me about San Antonio.

"We left here and got a ways out of town. That darn cannon wagon wasn't workin'. We kept tryin' to grease her up, but something didn't fit right. So Austin said to let it go. They took the barrel off the wagon and buried it deep as they could dig. Then, we put the cannon wagon over it and burned it. Looked like an Indian fire. Anybody'd think Indians took it from us. Won't nobody dig under a campfire like that, we didn't suppose.

"John, now think about it. All that fuss made over that cannon, and then it just ended up buried in the ground."

"Buried, but not taken from us. That was the point, Sydnie. And while all that was going on, some scouts were out counting the Mexicans. They found one feller in the brush, and figured it was a Mexican. But, no, it was a man by name of Ben Milam. He escaped from a Mexican jail. He'd been walking back, mostly at night so's he wouldn't be seen."

I shook my head, trying to imagine walking at night that way, considering the snakes. I was remembering my earliest nights in Gonzales.

"By then, we figure those lances weren't gonna help us much, since we'd be depending on our rifles. We made a ceremony and left them at Sandie's Creek. Ol' Milam was just watchin' us, and restin' up from his trials. Then we got word to meet some fellers at Cibolo Creek. We went on over there for a few days just to get word from the scouts. There's a lot of scouts, Sydna. There's so much going on, those fellers bring in important news every day. They're out in the woods, and they track the Mexican troops. There must be hundreds in the woods, just all over."

"Oh, my." I looked around toward the window wondering if scouts or Mexican troops might have eyes on our place.

"So, after a few days, we left Cibolo Creek. Next we stopped at Salado Creek." He sat up, rubbing his left knee. "Austin and the other leaders were disagreeing about what to do. So, we just waited for instructions." He was trying to remove his boots, but his left foot was too swollen.

I got up to help him, and with a great effort the foot finally emerged from the worn-out leather boot. We slipped the other foot out more easily, and John leaned on his elbows.

"They finally decided it was time for us to move on toward San Antone."

He laid back down, and I gave him a pillow from the bedroll.

"So, finally we got to the edge of the village. Then it was an argument about when to go in and how to go." He turned his head and looked at the ceiling of the cabin. "It was real confusing for a few days. We didn't know who was in charge, or what we were gonna do. So, they sent out scouts to count how many Mexicans they could find. While those scouts were out there, somebody brought a message to Austin. That committee meeting your daddy went to, they sent word for Austin to go to Washington, D.C. for help.

I was caught up in the idea of my Daddy's committee in a town to the east and how it could impact the volunteers in the woods far west of us. "Isn't that something, John? They got a message to you all the way from San Felipe."

"They sure did. And that sounded right to us, thinkin' we'd get some help. So, Austin said we had to vote for a leader while he's gone. We voted and chose Burleson."

"Do I know this Mr. Burleson, John? I can't place him." I was trying to follow his story and imagine all the men.

"No, Syd, you don't know him. He was from north of here. He's had lots of soldiering. He's a real cautious type. We figured that was a good thing."

I nodded my head to agree. I thought caution was a very good thing those days.

"Austin left, and we were waiting for the scouts to come back. Well, Milam, he can't sit still, so he volunteered to go scout for a while. And Burleson, he wasn't keen on going anywhere. Lots of men started leaving. They were bored. They came to fight, but if no fighting was needed, they were going back home to their families."

John put his hands out toward me, and I moved closer to him.

"Syd, I thought about you then. I really did. Trapper and me started to pack, to come back home." He laughed and leaned back on his elbows.

"You mean some men just left?" I asked.

"Yes, ma'am, they just left. And I was ready to do the same. But then Milam came in from his scouting. And Milam, he said we needed to go on to San Antone. He went in Burleson's tent and we heard arguing. Then when he came out, he asked who was going with him to San Antone. Me and Trapper said we'd go, and most everybody agreed they'd all go."

I sank back, realizing how close he had come to being home weeks ago.

"Milam just took over and told us how it would be. He put us in three groups. One group went ahead to make a distraction. They shot off their rifles to get the Mexicans away from town. Sure enough they all took their weapons and ran in the direction of the rifle fire. Then while they were going away from town, the

Lancers—we were all in one squad—we started into the town going down Acequia Street. The other squad went along another street." He winced in pain and lay back down on the bench.

"You want another pillow, John?" I brought it before he could answer. He took the pillow and put it under his injured leg.

"We made our way into town. We got near to the town square. Then we heard a commotion. Those Mexicans figured out they'd been bluffed, and they were coming back." He winked his eye, put his hands behind his head, and looked up at the ceiling. "I was scared to death."

He was quiet for a minute, and I just waited.

"Then Trapper saw a ladder. Like outta the blue, a ladder going up to the top of a house." He sat up and looked at me. "You know, Syd. They make those houses with mud. The walls are so thick, and you can't hardly knock a hole in it. And there's a little crown around the top of the house. So, we decided to go up that ladder. We just went on up and sat on that roof, behind that little crown. We saw other guys were on the other roofs, so we figured we done a smart thing. We stayed up there for four days."

He lay back down and looked up at the ceiling again. He closed his eyes and seemed to be reliving the episode on the roof. I wondered how much he'd had to eat and drink in the last few weeks.

"Can I bring you some water, John?"

"Oh, that'd be so wonderful."

I got the tin dipper and filled it with icy rain water. He sat up and drank it down. Then he wiped his mouth on his shirt sleeve.

"Aaah, that was really good, Syd. Thank you." He lay back down.

"Do you want some more?"

"No, just sit here with me. I want to tell you how it was." His eyes were closed.

"OK, John. I'm here." I took his hand.

He turned his head and looked at me. His face was ruddier than I remembered, and the muscles in his neck were taut. "About the middle of the second day, we felt hungry. Trapper had some dried beef he stashed from the Salado camp. So, we had a little of that. The fear sort of took our appetite away, you know?"

I really didn't know, and I really couldn't imagine. But I smiled and nodded that I accepted what he told me, and he went on.

"Then, the Mexicans came back into town, and some were coming up Acequia Street. We realized the Mexican sharpshooters from the church tower could see us. So we just had to stay in the shadows and stay still as we could." He looked back at me. "I didn't want to shoot anybody. After all that talk, when it came right down to it, I didn't want to shoot anybody. But we knew we were gonna have to if we were gonna survive. And we knew the whole point of our being there was to send those Mexican soldiers back to Mexico City."

John got up from the bench and walked over to the bedroll. He knelt down and started to unroll the bed.

"Here, John, let's make you comfortable." I handed him one of the pillows. He sat on the pallet and continued his story.

"Fortunately there was a tree limb over the roof. We got under there and propped our rifles in little valleys of the crown on top of the house." He ran his hand over a lump in the bed. "We said we'd cover each other for reload and switch off if we had to shoot." He crawled onto the bedroll and lay down with his hand on his forehead. "So that's what we did. For three more days we just watched, waited, and shot as we had to." He was quiet for a minute.

I took the other pillow and snuggled beside him.

"I think we shot five, Syd. Five. I don't really know." Staring at the ceiling, he paused as if looking down from the roof again in San Antonio. "We were up there on the roof for four days. Those three nights were the worst. It was so cold. In the quiet times I remembered how near I was to coming home." He looked at me and put his hand on my neck. "If the scouts would have come an hour later, I would have been on my way home. But there I was, on top of a Mexican house, shootin' my rifle at Mexicans in uniform." He looked away and shook his head.

"Are you hungry?" I offered him some bread and dried sausage I had in the cupboard.

"No, Syd. I'll eat tomorrow. I want to tell you all of it." He sat up again on the bedroll. "Finally, Trapper noticed the flag on the roof of the mission. It was coming down. And in a bit, they ran up a white cloth. Pure white." He was lost in remembering the whiteness of the surrender flag. "They gave up, Syd."

I smiled, thinking what a relief it must have been to all the Texians to see that white flag. But the story wasn't over.

"So, we wanted to come down from the roof. Cautiously, not sure, cause we still heard shots. We went to the place where the ladder was, but it was gone! We heard voices in English. So we thought we'd just jump. And that's when it happened. I went first and snapped my ankle. Trapper fell right on top of me," he said with an insincere laugh.

"So, Trapper helped me up, and we made our way to where the others were. Our men came around in the street, and we all walked together, watchin' to give cover. Then we found out Milam was dead. We couldn't believe it. Shot in the head." John's eyes seemed far away.

"We got everyone together and took count. Everybody accounted for everybody else. We buried Milam and gathered up our few dead. I didn't feel good about it, Syd." He turned away from me. "We killed a lot of Mexicans. I guess I should have felt good about it, but I didn't. With all those dead men, I couldn't give my leg much care. Considering everything, it's really nothing." He rubbed his leg a bit.

He was quiet for a long while. In the silence, I was lost for words to console a man who had killed, buried, and now regretted it.

He just wanted to make peace in Gonzales. I wondered if the killing in San Antonio was going to make any difference.

He remembered the events after the killing. "They talked for days about the conditions for release, or if we would take prisoners. We got to rest and eat. The town fed us good, and they celebrated. The people in that town were so happy to see that Mexican Army leave. Things were better for us."

"The Mexicans were headquartered in an old mission near the town square. It's about to fall apart, old as dirt. They took it from Spain and used it for a hospital. So they all met in there." My husband's words came slowly, as from a very tired man.

"We gave 'em a generous deal, I think. We agreed to let 'em stay till their wounded could travel. But we took that little mission, and Burleson gathered up all the weapons and anything their army had. They don't have a headquarters there now. It's ours, and that should keep 'em out of San Antone. Captain Neill stayed there in control of that mission they call the Alamo de Parras. Their commander was a general named Cos. He agreed to go back across the Rio Bravo. My understanding is they are not supposed to come back. Not ever."

John Benjamin looked at me with pleading eyes. "Could it finally be over, Syd? Did we do enough?" He got up and hobbled to the door. He opened it and stood in the opening, looking down the road to Gonzales. "People been angry ever since I got here, Syd. But I haven't been here very long. We were supposed to find a good life here."

I tucked myself under my husband's left arm and looked down the road with him. The baby in my belly had grown considerably while he was gone. John Benjamin gave my rounded middle a soft little pat. "Maybe we can have peace now, Syd."

We stood in the door for a long while. I remembered the joy we had in the year we courted. I hoped it would be that way again.

In the weeks that followed, skirmishes between Mexico and the settlers broke out all over the territory, and the score was fairly even. But the Gonzales battle for the cannon and the Gonzales Lancers' successful campaign with Ben Milam were two victories that made the men of Gonzales feel invincible. The fears and the shame were never again discussed in our cabin. The battles became glorified as both events were retold and celebrated in our little town. We heard it all from the triumphant participants. The Mexicans had gone home, and the gringos had won the day.

The adventure lovers by whose confidence northern Mexico was being redesigned were swindled by their own successes. After their two victories, they thought they couldn't lose. But they were dead wrong.

Morning, December 15, 1835 – Daddy D. Reflects on the Consultation in San Felipe

While the Gonzales Lancers were fighting with Ben Milam to kick the Mexican Army out of San Antonio, my daddy went to meet with other men from all over the Coahuila territory. They met out near the Brazos River in the heart of Austin's settlement in the village of San Felipe. Our silence was broken. It was time to discuss more drastic measures for getting proper titles to our land. Some folks even went so far as to say we should break away from Mexico.

Mexico was aware of our attitude. Everyone knew that acts of disloyalty could land a man in prison. Discretion was needed. There would be no convention. No, that would be treason. After all, the men were just consulting with each other. The meeting would be called a Consultation.

As head of our local committee, Daddy packed a saddle bag and left with some others from Gonzales. Representatives from all over the Coahuila territory converged on the little town of San

Felipe. Daddy was gone a month. He arrived back in Gonzales two days after Trapper Cain and John Benjamin rode in.

I was at my mama's cabin minding Eugene that mid-December day. I recognized that serious look on Daddy's face when he walked up our cabin step. He didn't even come in. Daddy stayed out on the trot and sat on the bench he made for us just a few years before. I watched through the window as my mother went to him. He stood up, pulled her close to him, and gave her a long hug. Then they sat again. Mother wanted him to rest. Daddy's eyes surveyed the yard, and then the street and the neighboring cabins. He ran his hand over the wood at the corner of the house and looked at the half-doors he designed. He nodded his head as if approving of his labor for the past five years, as if confirming the rightness of what he had accomplished so far.

"How did we come to this, Rebecca? How did I come from Green River Inn to be a rebel against the nation of Mexico?" He turned and gave her a forced smile. They sat. He leaned back against the house with his eyes closed.

"It could get bad, Becka," he continued.

"What do you mean, George?"

Daddy's answer came too slowly. Mother pressed him. Then he spoke softly with genuine reflection. Looking around the place again and not at her he said, "We could be in for a real war, and we could lose it all." He smiled a sad smile. "I never have gotten around to the hides."

"War." Mother repeated as if wanting to understand the context in his statement. Was it just a figure of speech, or did he really mean war?

"Another war," he explained. "That's all you can call it, if push comes to shove. We discussed what we wanted. We just want the rights we were promised," he said. "That constitution says everyone gets representation. We don't have representation, and we don't have proper papers. People need papers for their land. And we need protection. That's what was promised, and that's all we want. Everyone at the meeting agreed; it's very simple. We'll have our rights, either from Mexico or with Texas's independence from Mexico."

Daddy took a deep breath and began to explain what had been decided. "We have to meet again to put the papers together, Becka. They want to meet again in March. When that happens, the Mexicans won't like it. There'll be trouble. So, to get ready for that, we're forming an army."

"Oh?" Mother looked at him waiting for details. I was re-membering about the soldiering my husband just described to me a few days before.

"Yes, we all agreed. We have a general to take that on. A fel-la' named Houston was with us, and he can do it. He wanted to do it. We need volunteers to just hold onto what we got." Daddy stopped.

Mama waited for more.

"Houston says Gonzales is the best place for his headquarters, for anyone who wants to enlist to come here. Everyone is going back to their towns to spread the word and to get volunteers for the army to come here to sign on. Houston will come and make an office here. It's going to be something," he said as he turned a tired, serious face to my mama. "Everything is set. If the Mexicans refuse our rights, we have no choice. We can't continue to live like this, just squatters with no firm hold on our land, no help against Indian raids. We got Henry Smith lined up to be the temporary governor. With Houston and Austin, we'll do all right."

The men of the Consultation had wasted no breath on idle chat. Their time had resulted in decisive action. The Texians would stand their ground, starting in Gonzales.

I backed away from the window and sat on the bed. I imag-ined for a few minutes how it might be; my brother and my hus-band were exactly the right age for soldiering. I put my hand on my belly, got up, and walked to our cabin out on the Kellogg farm to discuss war with my husband.

Part 4:

Preparing for War

Afternoon, December 15, 1835 – Discussion of War

"John Benjamin, Daddy says there might be a war, and the town's gonna be run over with people coming soon to sign up with some general," I said in between gasps of breath after I practically ran to the house.

My husband was leaning over the rain barrel with a dipperful of drinking water. He took a long, slow drink and then stood up straight, looking at me with his mouth open, letting the notion of my news sort of leak down into his head.

"Well, we gonna go see 'bout this." He wiped his face with the back of his sleeve, took me by the arm and we started walking back to town. "Now, you tell me again, what did he say?"

I tried to explain it to him for the entire half mile, but he had too many questions and I had too little understanding.

"You're just gonna have to ask for yourself, John. I don't know anything except what he said to Mama."

My parents were still sitting on the trot, right where I left them earlier in the day. My brother John Gaston joined us. Mama put Eugene on her lap, and the five of us listened to Daddy describe the possibilities that lay ahead. After the cannon was buried in our own back yard, we understood how personal politics had evolved in Gonzales.

"We saw folks heading north," Daddy said. "Can't say I blame them, but if we're gonna live here, we need laws and proper papers."

"Sydna came home talking about war. Now what are you talking about?" John Benjamin asked him. "We just came back from San Antone and sent them Mexicans back to the Rio Bravo. We made a deal. I thought all this was settled!"

"Well, now anything is possible. There's been a lot going on up in Austin's settlement while you men were in San Antonio. We made a plan. First, we're just asking for what they already promised—our papers and some protection. If that doesn't come, we'll declare ourselves free. You know they won't accept that. There'll be some fighting going on."

John Gaston looked at John Benjamin. My husband just looked at my daddy.

Daddy continued talking. "General Houston is organizing an army right away. First, we need to hold that ground you men took in San Antonio."

John Benjamin took a deep breath and crossed his arms over his chest. "They said they're not coming back." Everyone was quiet. "Neill's down there with some troops, and he kept all their weapons."

"You men must have done a good job. And we sure hope they don't come back. But, just to be prepared, we've got to fortify. Houston says Gonzales is the best place to organize troops. This town is going to be full of volunteers. The men will come, and some will bring their families with them. Could be hundreds will come. We'll take them all." Daddy once again looked like a man wondering about the future, having more questions than answers.

John Benjamin looked at me with a troubled stare. Maybe it wasn't over after all. If running the Mexicans out of San Antonio hadn't stopped them, there would be more fighting before we'd have peace.

The delegates from the San Felipe Consultation were back home in every settlement across the entire Coahuila territory encouraging men to join Houston's army with the expectation of war. And if they wanted to join up, they'd all come to Gonzales.

Meanwhile in San Antonio, Captain James Neill was left holding the little mission where John Benjamin and Trapper Cain saw the white flag. It wasn't much, but the Texians would have a toehold if they held onto it. Mr. Austin, General Houston, and the delegates from San Felipe wanted it held. Captain Neill would stay at the Alamo de Parras and wait for help.

All this news of war was becoming too much for some families. Settlers who couldn't face any more stress were giving up on the Mexican promise. They took to the roads heading north, back to the United States.

Sure enough, within a few weeks, throngs of volunteers wanting to join Houston's army began to arrive in Gonzales. Mr. Austin had gotten word of our problems to President Jackson in Washington. Units from Kentucky, Tennessee, Georgia, and other state militia began camping all around us.

December 20, 1835 – The Heberts from Louisiana; Susie Castleware is Murdered

"John Benjamin, wake up. There is somebody outside!"

He pulled on his trousers and lifted the cover of a window. Outside our home in the thin early morning light were twenty-plus men. Some were walking; some rode horses. John stepped in the doorway and asked what he could do for them.

A tall, beanpole of a man stepped forward, removed his hat, and held it over his chest.

"We just need a campground, if you don't mind. We saw your field out beyond yonder and thought to ask permission to make a camp there till we can join up with Houston. The place looked so friendly, we took a notion you might be of a mind to let us camp here." He waited for an answer.

John looked at me behind the door. I was grinning, thinking about my place looking friendly. Privately I felt really proud.

John Benjamin winked at me and closed the door. He walked out toward the field behind the house. I peeked out from the window and listened to what they said. "Well, I'm John Benjamin Kellogg, and this is all part of my family claim. You can have a space out away from the house, up along the tree line." He pointed a ways out. "Stay outta the fields. And I don't want any bother for my wife here. That suits you, it'll be okay by me. But don't come up here," he said with a firm tone.

The man dipped his shoulder slightly and put out his hand. John took his hand and shook it the way men do.

"Much obliged, Mister Kellogg. I'm Hebert, Bartley Hebert out of Louisiana." He pronounced his last name like *aye-bare*. "These are my kin." He motioned with his hat to the crowd of men waiting to camp.

John stepped back and studied the faces of the men. There was a thread of resemblance among them with their long faces and narrow noses. There was not an ounce of fat among the whole lot. They had wide shoulders and olive skin, and they all moved slowly.

"These are *all* your kin?" John asked.

"Most all," Hebert said. Then he began to introduce them. "Chaney Hebert, Kirby Hebert, and Joel Hebert." He continued naming the men in the crowd. Then he stopped. There were about six men left to be named. Bartley Hebert looked at them, turned to my husband, and explained. "I guess these ain't all really kin but seem like kin since they come from our place over there in Louisiana. They're all kin so far as I'm concerned. I'll vouch for them all if I need to. We're all going to join up with the general as soon as he lets us. If it's okay by you, then we'll go put up our camp now."

Slowly, John Benjamin began to nod his head. "Yes, then. That's what you do. Just keep in your camp space, and we'll get along just fine."

"Much obliged." Hebert walked toward the tree line that edged the field.

The other men thanked John in chorus, some tipping their hats.

John came in. "We can do that much to help," he said, "but you beware."

The Heberts from Louisiana who camped on Kellogg land turned out to be honorable men. In fact, they posted themselves as sentries around to guard the place. They protected our property and assured John they wouldn't tolerate any violations so long as they were camped there. They could tell John every rabbit and squirrel that crossed the road, and they certainly took notice of any men that came around. We felt comfortable with them but hoped it wouldn't last that way for long.

The fields around us were dotted with tents, their fires glowing in the night. Recruits were encouraged to move on to help Neill hold the mission in San Antonio. Some took that option. A few took their families with them. Others left their families in Gonzales. As long as the Kellogg farm hosted the regiment from Louisiana, I went to town every day to avoid them. Town bustled with activity. It felt like the world was becoming very small. Every face I met was a potential brother or sister in the family of Texian patriots.

As in every family, there were problems. People of all persuasions came in and out of Gonzales every day. The situation was a fertile ground for trouble. Spies eking out a bit of information disguised themselves as patriots. Bounty hunters trickled in from the lawless frontier and had no patience for town. Men who came to fight were getting impatient, and they would find something to fight about.

Very near the end of the year, Susie Castleware was found dead in her cabin. She was the young wife of one of the volunteers who went to help Captain Neill hold the Alamo. She had been smothered. A feather pillow covered her face when she was discovered. From the marks on her body, it was clear she had been assaulted. The death continued to be an unsolved mystery, and the townspeople began to grow more suspicious and resentful of our role as host of the new army. We all hoped Houston would soon come and take his troops away.

"It's as bad as a Comanche raid!" a neighbor complained to my daddy. "There's nowhere safe, not even in town."

Friends of the couple went to fetch young Castleware from San Antonio. The news hit so hard, several other men came back for their families. Some mothers with children packed up and went with their husbands back to the mission. Other men chose desertion, joining the travelers going back north to the United States. Difficult choices had to be made. Everyone had to decide the best for his own family.

The chaotic year of 1835 finally came to an end. January of '36 brought us the hope of better times.

February 1, 1836 – David Crockett and Juan Seguin Come Through Gonzales

In early February, a man entered town wearing fringed buckskin. He needed no introduction. David Crocket was preceded by his reputation as a fierce fighter, a three-term congressman from Tennessee, and a man with an ambitious heart. He was famous all the way from the stage of New York City, where a play was produced about his life. Betrayed by political friends, he came to Texas to move on with his life. He'd been in Mexico for a while, philosophizing and declaring his affection for Tejas. He was in San Felipe when Daddy went there for the Consultation, and everyone knew he was on his way to San Antonio to help Captain Neill.

Mr. Crocket and a small group of Tennessee Volunteers stopped at the tavern. One of our local citizens immediately recognized him, and his companions confirmed his identity. I wasn't there, but to hear Nita tell it, he must have been an inspiration.

"He opened the door and called to his men. He told them to order-up and eat hearty," she said. "It was late in the afternoon. Everyone cheered him and wanted him to play his fiddle. So, he played, and they all danced. It was a good time," she said.

His celebrity bolstered the spirits of everyone in Gonzales, homefolks and enlistees alike. The group from Tennessee made a camp outside of town, and said they'd wait for Houston there. We could feel a new energy fanning the cedar elms around town. What was once fear and panic began to feel more like confidence.

As we were spellbound with the celebrity of Crockett, Juan Seguin returned to town with news only a spy could know. Seguin was a Tejano. He could travel like a chameleon all over the territory without being recognized. He frequented the saloons of San Antonio and was as comfortable in the cantinas of deepest Mexico. Juan Seguin could learn a lot by just quietly being around.

Covered with a week of dust and smelling of good Mexican beer, Seguin lighted in the tavern just long enough to describe his latest observation. "Santa Anna is garrisoned in Saltillo, and he is building his forces. He looks to San Antonio with hungry eyes."

With that information, David Crockett took his volunteers to help Captain Neill in the Alamo. Juan Seguin followed close behind.

February 24, 1836 – Camp Followers Come Back from San Antonio

As February came to an end, a small group of women came into Gonzales on the road from San Antonio. They were the wives of the men in the Alamo, and they brought their children with them. Nita called them soldaderas. She told me these camp followers washed clothes for their husbands, and they cooked the army rations. They served as nurses for the men who were sick. But now conditions there were intolerable, and they had given up their jobs as helpers. Their only support was the military payroll, which was not being delivered, and they had nowhere else to go. The women were haggard and dirty. The children were sick and hungry. They assured us the Alamo was the least agreeable place.

"The smell in that place made me sick. The food is rotting, and it smells something terrible," one woman said. "Thank God for the good water well. At least the children could wash, and we had water to drink. We took our relief in the pots and tossed it from the walls. We slept with the animals. The horses, a few cows, and some hogs were in stalls right there with the men. There was no more food brought in. What little we brought was gone or turning rancid. Finally we slaughtered the last hog. They wouldn't sacrifice the last milk cow, but when we left everything was used up."

Another woman explained that army supplies—or supplies of any kind—never arrived. The supply lines were being intercepted by Mexican troops still lurking in the woods. Without supplies the men had no way to continue their work. But there was plenty of corn liquor somehow being smuggled in from San Antonio. The soldiers had lots of reasons to be disillusioned, so they were drinking their miseries away. The aroma of alcohol, bodily fluids, and animal dung drifted in the stale air. The women were heartsick to see their children in such a place. They had no means to help the men anymore. They brought the children out of the unhealthy circumstances, walking all those miles in hopes of finding some mercy in Gonzales.

"General Houston needs to go now, go to help the men in the mission," said one.

"What good are they doing here, just standing around? What are they waiting for?" another protested.

The others agreed and chimed in with complaints of their own.

The women told us about the activities in the little mission called the Alamo. They explained that Captain Neill had been called away for a family emergency, and in his place a Colonel Travis was in charge. They explained what they observed, and why they were concerned.

"One man every day went up the corner, to a high place, so he could see a long way off. They didn't like it, but it had to be done. And when they came down, they told Colonel Travis what they saw. Mostly it was nothing. But a few days ago it was important news. The man said he saw the Mexicans. Travis said he didn't think so, but we didn't take that chance. We got our little ones and left."

It was this report from the women that gave us our first alert of the real trouble.

February 25, 1836 – Travis's Letter Arrives; "Victory or Death"

On February twenty-fifth, the day after the women and children described the conditions inside the Alamo, Dr. John Sutherland and a companion stormed into Gonzales. Sutherland dismounted in a hurry, though his leg was broken, and he hobbled with it splinted. The two men rushed up the boardwalk without even tying their horses. My brother saw them from the blacksmith shop as they hustled directly into Ponton's office. C.J. Schmidt and John Gaston went to secure the wandering horses.

In a few minutes, Ponton came out on the boardwalk in front of his land office. He called out to anyone who would listen. He stepped into the street. "Stop and listen!" He shouted. He pleaded, turning to each man who passed, "We can't wait any longer!"

He said as the crowd gathered, "Travis is under attack. He needs men now; he can't wait for Houston."

Tom Miller came out into the street to see what the commotion was about. While they were talking, another rider came in a cloud of dust. It was Albert Martin carrying a letter from Travis. Tom took the letter and read it. Travis was desperate for help. His letter closed with the words, "Victory or Death."

Tom dropped his hand to his side and looked around him. My brother and C.J. Schmidt were standing in the crowded street where they tied the two horses. "Gaston, you take a horse and go tell every man you can find to come here right away. We'll go to Travis in the morning."

John Gaston took the paper from Tom's hand and read the request from Travis. The Mexican Army was shelling the Alamo. Travis's men were greatly outnumbered with more enemy soldiers arriving by the hour. The men in the mission could not hold them off alone. Travis's appeal was intended for every village in the northern territory.

C.J. Schmidt saddled his favorite horse and led it to John Gaston.

"Tell everyone you can, son," Schmidt said as he handed the leather reins to my brother. "Tell 'em to come to the courthouse and I'll be there to meet 'em."

John Gaston went through the streets of Gonzales shouting, "Come to the courthouse and join the troops! Come out as soon as you can! Go to the courthouse!"

He made his way out to the Dodson farm. Ned mounted a yellow stallion bareback. The two friends took separate roads and alerted farm after farm throughout the territory before the sun went down.

February 26, 1836 – Gonzales Men Leave to Help Travis at the Alamo

The Gonzales men were inspired. Here was another justifiable opportunity to fight, and maybe with one more effort they would free us from Mexico's aggression. They'd held onto the cannon and followed Ben Milam to victory. Now they felt they were unbeatable. They were to form an honor guard of sorts, going on to San Antonio as the Gonzales Regiment even before Sam Houston's army could be ready. They started grabbing things, packing their horses, slapping each other on the back, and hollering about how they'd "whipped-up on those Mexicans before, and they could sure do it again."

I didn't like to hear that kind of talk. I went with John Benjamin to our cabin so he could pack his things. "Did you forget, John Benjamin? Mac and Nita are Mexicans. Juan Seguin is as Mexican as they come. They are all fine people. We couldn't survive here without them. They want peace just like any of us. It's not the Mexican people, it's the Mexican government that went back on their promises to us. It was the Mexican government who put Mr. Austin in prison. Why, this little village is even named after a Mexican. How can you men talk so ugly about the Mexicans?"

John sat down and thought for a moment. "Sydna, you're right. There is a difference between the Mexican people and the Mexican government. If we look around, we'd have to admit there are a lot of Mexican people who are working as hard as anyone to civilize this country. But they're called Tejano, not Mexican. And they aren't getting their papers, either." He pulled on one boot. "Juan Seguin is committed to decent living around here. He has a whole pack of spies we've been depending on for at least a year now. But those Mexican soldiers and Santa Anna's officers have to be stopped. I'm tired of their lies and manipulations."

I watched him put on the second boot and stand up, as if his leg had never been injured.

"We've tried to get help through the law, Sydna. I thought this was over, but it's not."

He hugged me, and I knew he was acting for the good of our little family and for all of Gonzales.

Some Gonzales men rode off to Goliad and to the Brazos territory to get more help. There was an expectation that surely, hundreds—maybe thousands—of men would arrive down there at that mission in a few days. But these men from Gonzales were possessed by that familiar spirit. They couldn't wait to go and finish their job.

I stood there with my mouth gaping open in a state of disbelief. "You don't have to go, you know, John Benjamin. You went before. You have a baby coming." I protested, but it did no good.

"Don't you worry, Sydna. We'll take care of this and be back before that baby comes," he assured me as he threw his gear in his saddle bags. He turned to me, took my head in his hands, looked me in the eye and explained. "We're going to finish this thing. We'll all be better for it one day. Mac and Nita, you and me and our baby—we'll all have a better life."

"I believe you," I answered as he turned to leave.

All the men left, not even looking back.

I walked to my mama's cabin.

"Are you going, Daddy?"

He motioned me into the house as he and Pop Kellogg talked together in the yard. Neither was enthusiastic about physical confrontation. They loved work, but fighting was not in them. They were better at negotiations, and they knew their limitations.

Daddy came in and explained. "There's all sorts of trouble in town these days. We still don't know who killed the Castleware woman. Kellogg and I are old, and probably not as fit as the others wanting to go. The town needs some men to stay here. We'll be more useful watching out for the town and helping take care of the women left behind."

And with that, they went back to their work.

I had mixed emotions about it. I knew I didn't want any of them to go. Nothing was clear, and nothing made sense. I just accepted it as part of the confusion.

At the same time Gonzales men were organizing to go to San Antonio, others in town were packing to go back to a convention in the Brazos River Valley. The local officials met and decided that Daddy wouldn't go to San Felipe this time. He was needed to try to maintain some order in town. He had done his part at the Consultation, and others would go to help write the official papers.

A few days after they all left, March came in with freezing rain. The town was crowded with men enlisting for Houston's army, anticipating their advance to the southwest. Only the thirty-two-man Gonzales Regiment of volunteers had gone at the end of February, expecting Houston's New Texas Army and more volunteers to join them soon.

From the minute Doc Sutherland and Albert Martin came to town, something was unsettled in my soul. I couldn't get warm. An anxiety teased at me. Each day seemed more troubling than the last. The rain, the mud, and cloudy skies all day long bothered me. Of course, it was near my time to have the baby, and I was anxious because my previous experience with motherhood had not gone well. With John Benjamin and my brother gone and the Hebert men camped on our land, I moved back into my mother's house on St. Louis Street. I wanted to be with family and to be close enough for any news that came into town. I was sure glad my Daddy and Pop Kellogg were at home.

March 6, 1836 – A Storm is Brewing in the Distance (Fall of the Alamo)

Early Sunday morning, I went back to my cabin to get some handwork. It didn't take long, and I immediately turned around to go back to town. Mud caked my shoes by the time I reached Mother's cabin. At the fence, my brother kept a shoe scraping tool he made for just such a job. I propped my bundle on the front step, turned, and walked the few steps back to the rail fence. Giving complete attention to the shoes and the mud, I barely noticed the flashes of light from the southwest. The accompanying sound of thunder got my attention. It was then that I took notice of a storm brewing in the distance. Mama's neighbor stopped working in her garden, and we looked for clarification in the direction of San Antonio.

"More rain coming," predicted a large enlistee, passing on the road. "Been lightning all night," he confirmed to those of us listening.

With that logic we turned our attention to the day ahead. It was March sixth. There was more than weather brewing in the southwest.

March 8, 1836 – A Very Special Doll

My brother, John Gaston, and my husband, John Benjamin, both went to San Antonio to help Colonel Travis in the mission called the Alamo. Tom Miller went, too, and Mr. Dickinson from the blacksmith shop. There was so much confusion I didn't know if C.J. went, but I believed he stayed to help in town.

Back in December, Tom had sold his hotel and store on Water Street. The new owner wanted Nita to continue to run the place because she knew her job so well. She needed help with all the extra people in town, and I had promised I would help her. I went over there as often as I could, but I soon realized my limitations. I couldn't do it. I had to leave most of it to Nita. Each day the effects of my pregnancy worsened. My belly got in the way. I couldn't catch my breath. My hands and legs were swollen.

On the morning of Tuesday, March eighth, I went to the store early to open before Nita came in. I planned to help her through the early morning rush of business. My foot slipped on a mud pile at the edge of the boardwalk and I went down with a thud. I got a terrible bruise on my arm and scratched my face.

"Sydna! What has happened to you?" Nita noticed my injuries as she came in the door.

"Just a fall, Nita."

"But you have the baby. You wait here, and I go get help. No arguing." In an instant she was gone.

Nita was right. A tooth had cut the inside of my lip, and my face was beginning to swell. My arm ached. I worried if the baby was injured, or if my delivery would be affected. I knew I needed to go back to Mama's, and I was thankful for my dear, wise friend.

I stayed just long enough for Nita to take a horse out to the Dodson farm and to bring Grace back. Before they could return, the store was buzzing with newcomers. They postponed their shopping while patiently commenting about my dirty, swollen face. I explained what happened, and they waited for Nita before making their purchases.

A woman came in wanting just a place to wait for her husband. She held the hand of her little daughter, and in the woman's arms she carried a doll. The doll was the size of a toddler. The body was fashioned of plain muslin. Expressive brown eyes were embroidered with heavy thread. A mop of hair was made from shreds of yellow fabric, each one sewed carefully to the muslin scalp. Happy yellow embroidered ducks swam on the faded lake of blue gingham that made the dress, complete with little sleeves. A slip of cotton eyelet peeked out from under the little skirt. Tiny little brown stockings covered the feet, secured with whip stitches to hold them to the little legs. A pair of leather shoes completed the replica of a well-loved child.

The doll was adorable, like nothing I had ever seen. I asked the woman how she came to acquire it. "Oh, this is my way of remembering," she said with obvious emotion. Then she composed herself a bit. "I couldn't bear to throw away these clothes. We lost our little Margaret when she was two." The woman looked at the face of the doll. "In my grief I made the doll and put these clothes on her."

Her story stunned me. I was a bit sorry I had asked about the doll, causing her to relive the pain. I knew that pain. I brought my shawl around to cover my rounded belly and I recovered my breath. Tears were filling my eyes. I forced myself to look away for a moment.

The woman bent down and gave the doll to her daughter. "Here, Salina. You hold Maggie for a while." She stood up and glanced toward my midsection. "God bless you, ma'am." Then she walked away.

The woman disappeared into the crowd of people. I watched her walk away, and I thought about the pain and heartache the settlers experienced here in the promised land of Mexico. Then I heard Grace Dodson call my name.

Nita and Grace took charge of the store, and I hurried back to St. Louis Street.

I was beginning to feel sort of achy in my back. As I cleared the doorway to her house, Mama expressed her concern over my obvious injuries. She boiled water and poured it into the big tub, pulling a curtain across a wire for my privacy. In the dark corner of the sleeping room I sank into a heated bath. It was the most luxurious experience I'd had in years. I just sat there in that hot water with my eyes closed, imagining our little family of three as we would be this time next year.

That soothing hot water made me remember John Benjamin's embrace, and I reminded myself to be patient. I wondered how the men in San Antonio were doing and how soon they would be back. We hadn't had any news since they left. I was sure they'd be back singing their own praises and bragging of another victory, any day now.

One of the treasures I brought from Kentucky was a robe handed down from Mama. It was comfortably broken in and felt a little like John Benjamin had his arms around me. When I wrapped myself in that thing, I remembered the sweet smells of the Green River Inn. It was a simple robe of soft cotton, fashioned with lace along a long lapel that wrapped from the waist around the neck and down to the waist again. It was cut generously. It fell to mid -calf, engulfing my body. I loved it and took great pleasure when I had occasion to wear it. This time of waiting for my child and waiting for my husband seemed like an appropriate time to indulge myself with this treasure.

I rose from the cooling water and wrapped myself in the robe. As I prepared to dress, my thoughts drifted again to my family.

The three men I watched leave for San Antonio in late February were my heroes long before the Alamo. First, John Gaston was my childhood hero. His smile lit up the room. He filled our days with laughter, and I turned to him when dread set in. His hands were always ready to help me when mine were too small or too weak. He was a gifted listener, and in his presence, my fears evaporated. It wasn't his words, but rather the reassuring silent expressions on his face that gave me confidence. We had shared our experiences on the boat, in our tent, under our warm covers, and in the woods by the river. His quiet strength sustained me. Because of my brother, our childhood was a happy one.

Tom Miller set me on a pedestal and gave me the highest comforts available in Gonzales. The respect of the community was extended to me because of him. He gave me a home, financial support, and a distinctiveness in town. We shared the loss of a child, and then recovered together enough to appreciate a simple life with our common friends. What I knew with Tom was bittersweet.

And then John Benjamin Kellogg valiantly lifted me out of my depression. When my soul was frozen like the ground that held my first baby, John Benjamin broke the ice and melted my heart. With him I felt young, strong, hopeful, and excited about life again. I visualized life beyond the dark days, far down the road of time, when we would all find ourselves as comfortable as we had been before Mexico. He would help fulfill my goal of true family love and human kindness.

I wanted them all back from San Antonio, each for a different reason.

I put on a big, heavy gown and slid into the old, familiar covers of my old bed. The house was eerily quiet inside. I remembered the days before there was a house, when we camped on the lot for the first time. I remembered the thrill of watching the house being built and the men who made that happen. Most of them were in San Antonio now. I thought about the card games I'd played with my brother in that house. In no time at all, I was asleep. In my dreams I saw the three men I loved, watching them once more, as they rode away the last time to San Antonio.

Then I heard the voices of men. Awakening from a good night of sleep, I opened my eyes as the sun was just coming up. It was the morning of a new day and there was a clamor outside. I praised the Lord, believing the Gonzales men had come home in the night. I went to the window and pulled back just the corner of the hide that covered the opening. I couldn't see enough to tell who was outside, but I could distinctly hear men's voices.

DeWitt Colony had by this time become a sizable army camp. The various brigade leaders had their troops camped on every hill and in every valley. Each unit maintained its own specific area.

There were units in the river bottom and units in the woods. There were two separate camps in town. Tents could be seen like tiny villages across the plains outside of town, just like the Hebert camp on our place. Hearing men shouting and having clusters of men meet in the streets was becoming normal. But I hoped the voices I heard this morning were those of our Gonzales men, home now to announce another victory.

I quickly dressed and went into the cooking room of Mama's cabin. Coffee and biscuits were on the stove. I took a cup of coffee and a biscuit out on the porch dividing the two main rooms of the cabin. I was feeling stiff from yesterday's fall, and my legs felt weak. I wasn't sure I'd keep that coffee down, but I nibbled on the biscuit and drank the coffee just because it was hot.

I was looking for my brother or John Benjamin. Now I could see the men's faces clearly. I didn't recognize any of them. Two older men came down our street on my side, so I went to the gate and asked if they were back from San Antonio.

"No, little lady, we ain't gone yet!" one of them said, politely lifting the curled, broad brim of a sweat-stained hat. "We're just getting outfitted and groupin' up. We'll go when Old Sam tells us."

"Old Sam is coming. He'll be here any day," another said.

They walked beyond Mama's place on into the town center to mingle in the crowds waiting for the general. I just stood there, disappointed, confused, and slowly accepting that it would be another day at least before our men would be back. Nausea was welling up in my stomach from the coffee. I went back into the house to wait.

March 10, 1836 – Two Old Men and General Houston

Waiting is a hard thing for some people, and I was one of those people. My mind and my fingers needed to be busy, even if my feet were still. I had a quilt I'd been working on since '34, so I spent the morning tacking the little squares. A clock in the cooking room was ticking like a heartbeat in the house. Each hour it beat out the time with a deep, mellow tone. I never took notice of it before, but today it sounded as loud as thunder.

The windows were covered to keep out the cold. Sounds from outside were muffled, but it sounded like the crowd was growing. My self-control was soon exhausted. When boredom and curiosity took over, I got dressed enough to be seen in town and walked myself over to the store on Water Street.

I'd never imagined such crowds in Gonzales. It was like being back on those strange streets of New Orleans. There was a buzz of energy, with men grouping up, comparing their long guns and horses, and parading up and down the street, asking each other which group they belonged to. I heard plenty of speculation about when General Houston would be there.

Women with their children were in town, too, shopping, and talking, and looking confused. The whole town was in a state of confusion. People were yelling, boots were thumping, horses were clopping, and the freezing rain was just pouring down on all of it, making the mud slosh. It was a mass of confused humanity in a miserable mudhole, trying as best as they could to prepare for a war.

When I forced my way through the crowd in front of the store, I just stood in disbelief. There was Grace in her trousers, organizing the crowd into three lines. Her boots were firmly planted on the wooden floor. With outstretched arms she was trying to make the people in the crowd take some orderly manner before they came into the store. Her forceful personality was working well for her. She let only six people go into the store at any one time. When one came out, the next could go in. And nobody got in without Grace's approval.

Nita and Mac were behind the bar collecting money and making change. I stood and watched, feeling dizzier and more nauseous as the moments passed. The thought of leaving without helping became a stabbing pain in my chest. My gut went tight, my back ached, and my knees were weak. I decided they really didn't need me.

I turned to leave, hoping my friends hadn't seen me. My ears started to ring, and my eyes failed me. I wanted to sit on the long bench outside the store front, but it was already full. I grabbed onto the end of the bench and held on tight as my eyes came back into focus.

A bearded, grizzly-looking man began pushing his way through the crowd. In his drunken state, he didn't realize he was required to get into one of the lines. His breath smelled rank, and each of his eyes looked in a different direction. He grabbed for the door frame and got my arm by mistake. He laughed garishly when he realized what he had done, and he fell down among all those people trying to be orderly. Grace saw us. She spread out her arms to protect me from the fallen man.

"You get!" she said to him. "You're not welcome here, now. Go on, get away from here."

The drunken man skulked away, and Grace helped me regain my balance.

"You okay, Sydna?" she asked.

"Sure, I'm fine. I just need to get to Mother's place," I told her. She nodded her head and helped me past the mob.

I hugged the outside wall of the store, walking along the boardwalk until there was no more wall to hug. I crossed the street and walked on to Mama's cabin. My body was drenched and chilled by the time I reached Mama's place. I was glad to see Mama in the cabin. She put extra wood on the fire. My wet clothes went to the floor, and I wrapped in my robe. Two dry, heavy stockings cuddled my legs. I sat down in front of the fire, and Mama gave me a cup of scalding hot willow tea.

Mother asked how I felt. By then I realized I really needed to consider the messages my body was giving me.

"I don't know, Mama. I just really don't know," I said. I was nine months pregnant. My husband was gone with his friends to San Antonio so they could fight the whole Mexican Army. The town was full of raunchy men. The homeless families of enlistees looked at me with needy eyes. I had mixed feelings about what Gonzales had become and how I was feeling. I went back to bed to work on my quilt.

About six in the evening, I heard Nita. Her voice was dark and dreary. I panicked, wondering what I would say. Was she hurt because she saw me leave without helping at the store when they were so overrun? She came to the bedside with a look I'd never seen on her beautiful face. Her big brown eyes were like liquid drops of chocolate. Her long hair was tied behind her neck, a few tendrils springing loose and sticking to the hairline. Her face was wet from the moist air outside. She was shivering and breathing heavy. Her hands were clenched together, trying to get warm.

I reached for her hands. "Nita, I'm so sorry, I—"

She interrupted me as she sat on the bed. No, she wasn't angry. She understood. She asked how I felt but seemed too preoccupied to really want an answer. I asked her how things were at the store.

"Closed," she said with a smile. Then her face went serious again. "Mister Houston finally came today, Sydna."

"Oh, that is wonderful, Nita. Finally. Maybe now he will take all these men and go to San Antonio. Maybe things will calm down!"

"I need to tell you what else happened today," she said. "Two old men came in asking for General Houston. Mac took them to find him. Mac says Mr. Houston put them in the jail overnight. He says their story doesn't make sense, and Houston doesn't believe them."

I waited for their story. What was the story the general didn't believe? "Why doesn't he believe them?" I pressed her.

"They are spies, Sydnie. They just want to see how many men Houston has here. If they go back to San Antonio, they will tell Santa Anna's men that we are getting ready for war. Houston told Ponton not to let them go until after he takes his troops on to San Antonio."

Nita's words still didn't make complete sense. She still hadn't told me the old men's story. "What did the men say, Nita? What did General Houston not believe?"

She stalled again, telling me about the crowds at the store. She stood up, rubbed her hands together, and began pacing. "Most of the supplies are sold out, and everything was left in shambles. All those people came in just grabbing and putting things wherever they wanted. The store is a mess. Maybe some traders will come soon with more supplies." She lifted the window cover. "I wonder how long it will be till Houston takes all these men on to San Antonio."

"Even when the men leave, we'll still have all the women and their children in town," I pointed out. "They'll need help until the men come back."

Nita gave me a nervous glance. "Most of the liquor is gone. We serve all those men in the tavern every night. The townspeople have donated all their vegetables and meat, and those soldiers are eating well. But if we run out of liquor, I don't know what they will do about that."

Her procrastinations were becoming more transparent. I wondered why she was avoiding the real topic of the two old men. Then she turned away and tilted her head, brushing her hair back from her face. The silence in the room was unnerving.

"Nita. You still didn't tell me. What did the old men say?"

Unable to avoid it any longer, she pulled up the little stool. She took my hands in hers and said, "Sydnie, we don't believe what they say. They are liars, just looking for information. They want us to believe … they tried to tell us … they said the Alamo is lost. But it can't be true. We would have heard by now."

The breath in my lungs wouldn't go in or out. I had to think about her words. I just looked at her.

"That's what they said."

"They are liars," I agreed. "If the Alamo was defeated, somebody would have come back to tell us."

She nodded. There was nothing else to say. It was agreed. With confidence that the two old men were liars, we each took a deep breath and shared a reassuring hug. It would get us through the next twenty-four hours.

Early Afternoon, March 12, 1836 – Mrs. Dickinson Arrives Back from the Alamo

Another day passed, and my condition was no better. I remember it was a day I stayed in the bed until noon, determined to finish that quilt before the baby came. My legs felt like dead weights. My jaw hurt, and my shoulder ached.

Nita appeared at my door in the afternoon. I thought she had taken ill. She was white as milk. Her lips were pale, and her mouth was so dry my name came out a whisper. She slowed as she approached my bed, just looking at me for a long while. I stared back at her. I shook my head and raised my hands gesturing, "What?" I wondered what on earth she was thinking.

Finally she spoke. "Oh, my God, Sydnie." She reached out and took the needle out of my hand. She put all my sewing things on the floor. Sitting on the low stool next to the bed, she took my hands in hers. "It was true." She said softly.

I refused to know what she meant. Trying to deceive myself, I asked her, "What are you talking about, Nita?" I began to shiver.

She dropped her head so her chin touched her chest. In a soft, low voice she whispered, "The mission, Sydnie." Then she raised her face and looked squarely into my eyes. "It was lost—days ago."

My eyes searched her face as her words formed an obstruction in my throat. Eventually some words came out of me in a low growl. "How do you know?" I needed to understand this impossibility.

Nita dropped to her knees next to my bed. "Sydnie, that man—the one who doesn't hear—he found Mrs. Dickinson with her little girl on the road from San Antonio. He brought them back to town late in the night. They had been with Santa Anna. The news is all over town."

She sat on the floor and took a staggered breath. She couldn't look at me as she told me the report just as she had heard it. Her voice was weak and monotone. With great pauses and forcing the words out from between her teeth, she told me, "He shot them all. He stacked them up like fire wood and burned them all in one big fire."

Then she lifted her face, and I could see where her tears had made their tracks. She continued. "Mrs. Dickinson saw it all. She says Santa Anna is coming for us."

I didn't want to know then. I needed to let her words trickle into my brain a little at a time. I was too stunned to speak. The events of the past few days were beginning to confirm what she was saying. The thunder we heard in the distance, and the flashes of lightning we saw on Sunday morning must have been cannons. And the two old men in the jail weren't liars after all.

I turned my legs to the side of the bed and put my feet on a cold floor. Nita stood with her hand over her mouth, sobbing. Finally I allowed myself to speak the only truth left to say. "They are never coming home."

Afternoon, March 12, 1836 – Packing up Gonzales

I sat on the bed feeling a cold breeze slipping in through the window. The truth was making its way into my mind. The clock I only recently noticed chimed four times. It was a death knell, honoring three grown men and the child who would never know them. I looked toward the clock and saw my mother standing in the doorway holding a faded, red, wool cap.

Mother was thinking of my brother. He was only seventeen, and had lived so little, really. The look on her ashen face was pain drenched in disbelief. The truth of what was happening cut into us. We were three stunned women, not knowing what to say. The shock was so deep I couldn't yet cry. We stood in reverence until my mother broke the silence.

"They say Santa Anna is coming for us. We have to leave here."

Leave? I thought. *Go where? How? My baby is coming. My husband is gone. How can we just leave?*

Nita gasped and dashed away. Mother came to where I was sitting. Little Eugene clung to her skirt, trying to understand all the sadness. Mother sat Eugene on her lap and took my hands in hers. She looked deep into my eyes as our souls connected. She was my mother, and she was the woman who shared my grief. She explained that Daddy and the Kelloggs were already packing the wagons.

"Your brother and John Benjamin … they're gone, Sydnie," she said bluntly. "But we don't have time to think about it now because if we do, we'll all be gone." She hugged Eugene and closed her eyes tight. "You take a minute or two to think about what you want to pack from your cabin, and you'll come with us. But we don't have much time."

My crippled mother stood up. Somewhere she found a new strength. She knelt down to face Eugene. She brushed his hair with her hands and took a long look into his eyes. She picked up her young son and carried him out of the room. Then I was alone.

I just sat there, letting the truth sink in. My mother had lost her darling son. She and Ma Kellogg had as much reason as me to crumble. But I knew we wouldn't. We couldn't. We had to take the little ones and leave.

Sounds of horror began to fill the town. Living in the middle of it, we could hear the thunder of horses' hooves, the rattle of buckboards and wagons, the booming urgency of the men's instructions, and the piercing, pitiful cries of the women and children. Mothers, wives, and children had lost sons, husbands, and fathers. Every family in the settlement had been represented in the Gonzales Regiment, and now every family shared their loss.

I took Eugene from Mother and went to the porch so she could concentrate on her decisions. There was very little time to decide what to take and how to pack it in the wagons. I didn't need anything from my cabin. My greatest treasures were already gone, and my future lived inside me.

Eugene was holding John's red cap. I took the cap and held it to my face for a moment. The smell of my brother filled my head with memories of Kentucky. I remembered the day I'd found this hat in the snow. We had a choice then, and we made our decision to come here. Now we would know the cost of that decision. But I didn't have time to deal with all that. I lifted Eugene to sit on the bench and handed him the cap. He hugged it to his little chest and looked at me.

"John?" he asked.

"Yes, John," I confirmed. I hugged him. "Our John is gone, Eugene."

"Gone?" he repeated. Of course, he wouldn't understand for a while, but for now it was all I could do to share the impossible truth aloud.

There on the trot between the main rooms of Mama's cabin, I heard the community of Gonzales begin to dismantle. Women were crying out in their grief. Children were asking why. Most of the women had no one else but their children now. I was realizing an irony that the two older men from my family, who stayed behind to take care of the women in town, would now be instrumental in saving their lives.

Many women were so despondent they couldn't attend to themselves or their children. They were in shock. Those who could think began to load wagons for those who could not. Some were literally running and throwing things together, while others were standing like stone, unable to function at all.

A woman was staggering on the road, walking back and forth, beating her chest with her crossed forearms. Her two children were sitting in a cold pool of rain water at the edge of the roadway, just crying and reaching up for anybody to comfort them. Then in a moment of amazing grace, I saw little Jessie.

The Carters had come to town. They had gotten word of the disaster. Mr. Carter was enlisting to go with the general, and they were waiting for instructions. Jessie was sitting in the wagon with Mrs. Carter, clean and wearing a new dress. Her hair was combed. She was plump with rosy cheeks. Her owl eyes were gone. Jessie had grown into a beautiful young lady with the dark, captivating eyes of one wise beyond her years.

She got out of the wagon, went to the children, and took each one by the hand. In her quiet and gentle way, she led them to our porch. Jessie sat next to me and put one child on each of her legs.

Mama shuffled out to help the children's mother. The woman came with Mama to our porch but remained detached. She sat on the bench, and Jessie took her children to her side. Then Jessie went back to wait with the woman who loved her.

Neighbors consoled each other, and through their tears, they tried to prepare to escape. But there was no escape from the horror.

I remembered the story from the Bible, the night the Death Angel passed through Egypt, killing a male in every family. Our Death Angel had already visited San Antonio and was on his way to Gonzales.

Enlistees gathered in the tavern to discuss their options. Nita and Mac were there. The last of the corn liquor was consumed without the need of a glass. Then General Houston rode out on his big, white stallion, looking like a king and sounding like God himself. He called out in a thunderous voice, just to establish his presence. The men all rushed into the street and a hush came over them. The burly mob all looked at their leader.

"These women need help getting ready to leave. They'll take everything they can. Bring all the supply wagons to the town center and load their things," he instructed. "Take heed for thorough preparations. Do what you can for the women, and then prepare the units for our departure."

As he continued to speak, it was soon clear he was not going to San Antonio. There was a murmur from the men. Some ducked their heads and took sideward glances at their companions. Houston insisted they would be slaughtered if they exposed themselves now. He instructed the leaders of the various regiments to ready themselves for a midnight muster. They would go east.

East? Yes, away from San Antonio. Houston said they needed to increase the army, or else the Mexicans would cut them down for sure. This didn't set well with men who felt so confident when the Mexicans agreed to go back across the Rio Bravo. Those men were now grumbling, privately calling Houston a coward. Someone shouted out, "Remember Ben Milam!" And then they did remember. Milam was dead, the result of his insistence to fight. Houston was in charge now, and he was not going the way of Ben Milam. There wasn't time to argue.

As the crowd gathered in the street, another man took their attention. The Methodist circuit preacher walked up to Houston's horse. The general looked at him and gave him a nod of approval. The Reverend Stephenson began to talk, but his voice was lost on the first few rows of the crowd. In an uncharacteristic show of patience and respect, the crowd waited as three men assembled a temporary podium to lift the pastor high enough to be heard across the crowd.

Preacher Stephenson stepped up to speak and the crowd fell silent. He said very few words, but they were exactly what the town needed to hear. He ended with a prayer for guidance and protection, and then he stepped down. Where there had been grumbling and doubts, there was at least a sense of duty, if not confidence. The men fell in line. They packed the women as best they could, and then they followed Houston out of town in the dark of night.

Before Dawn, March 13, 1836 – Burning Gonzales

Long before the sun rose, and after the army was gone, the women began to bury everything remaining in the cabins and barns. The few men left in town dug the holes while the women and children dumped in their precious belongings. "Anything useful needs to go," they said. "Take it or destroy it." Food, tools, clothing, kitchen wares, anything that wasn't packed would be buried. If it wasn't buried, it would be burned. Nothing would be left to enrich the approaching enemy.

Marmie Lane and her oldest daughter Sharon made torches so the town could see to work. It was an eerie sight. Movement was distorted in the artificial light, and the smoky shadows increased the sinister feeling of our awful predicament. The older children were told to make a final sweep of the buildings calling out to ensure no one was left behind. Everyone was yelling, banging things, and crying.

Young David Carpenter came by our fence. He was fortunately just too young to be in anybody's army but grown enough

176

now to be the man of his family. "What about the ducks?" he yelled out to his older sister, Myrtle.

She put her hand to her mouth, trying to think of how to spare the precious birds. "Bring Lollie, and shoo the rest of them to the woods," she cried out to him. "I don't want them to burn up."

Lollie was famous all over town for her eggs. She would leave with the rest of us. As the children ran to their duties, I remembered my own red rooster and two hens. I thought for a moment, and then I remembered. They weren't in the coop; they were loose. They had a chance. My little chickens would have to fend for themselves. I couldn't go back to John Benjamin's cabin.

Papa Kellogg brought around their buckboard. Daddy led Barley and pulled our wagon in line by the Kelloggs. I took Eugene, and we climbed into the back of the wagon. Daddy brought out our extra clothes and a basket of cooking pots. I lined the bottom of the wagon with the things we could take and just waited.

Nita found us and climbed in. "I want to ride with you a ways," she said. "Mac will bring our wagon at the end of the line."

Gonzales packed up overnight. Long before first light, there was a line of buggies, wagons, buckboards, oxen, horses, and women on foot making a caravan along Water Street. Wheelbarrows were packed, and bundles were tied on skids to be dragged away. Everyone formed a line, waiting for the women to finish destroying the town.

It was agreed to make our way east by traveling from river to river across the northern span of Tejas. The first leg would be to Mina on the Colorado, which was forty miles due north. That road was good and would take us the farthest distance in the shortest time.

Suddenly, we heard the swoosh of fire as it consumed its first breath of oxygen. Blazes flashed. Bundles of dry hay ignited. Women set their own homes ablaze. Every cabin and every barn would burn through the night.

I saw Daddy walking from the Kansteiner place with his torch. He was a silhouette against the blaze that consumed the barn the Comanche spared. I knew what he was going to do. With each of his steps, a scream released itself inside my head. I gritted my teeth. My fingernails cut into my palms as I clenched my fists. First, he went behind his house, and then he appeared with a bundle of small branches. Holding the flame to the branches, he set them ablaze. He walked onto the trot of Mama's cabin and opened the top of both doors. Into each room he tossed a flaming torch. He left the burning bundle of branches on top of the table on the trot and stepped away from his home. I couldn't watch any more. I couldn't bear to see the trot destroyed. I wanted to remember it the way it had been. I turned away like a coward.

I stayed in the back of our wagon. Nita was sitting on the seat where Daddy would sit to drive us away from Gonzales. She was watching them, telling me sadly as each unbelievable act was committed. Big Mac was helping the women. After a while he ran to us, panting and struggling for his breath. "We'll go soon," he said. "Just stay here and we'll go soon."

Of course we felt panicked, imagining the Mexican army would be arriving at any moment. Daddy came to check our wagon. Eugene stayed with me, still holding John's cap. He tucked his head and curled under my arm. He peeked out from under my sleeve with big, bright eyes. I believed the poor child was too frightened to speak.

Daddy crawled up onto the seat of the wagon, and Mama sat beside him. We waited. Nita sat beside me, and we huddled there together with my youngest brother. From out of the throng of noise, a woman's voice came from a distance. The wagon train took life.

As our wagon jolted forward, I heard what sounded like a hundred squeaking wheels and the sloshing of rain puddles. The mule snorted and there was a great, unfamiliar dirge created by an entire community in mourning.

Part 5:

The Runaway Scrape

March 14, 1836 – John Benjamin Kellogg III Is Born in the Wagon

There are times in life when the heart stands still, the brain ceases to function, and thoughts won't come. I was holding my breath until the full light of morning, only because I was too stunned to breathe. Facing the back of the wagon, I tried to organize some thoughts about what was happening to us. Nita pulled the canvas back. The musty smell of wet smoke was following us like dragon breath. Gonzales was no more. She had been lifted to heaven by the fires. What had taken years to build was gone in a matter of hours.

I kept thinking of all the women whose husbands were in the regiment of men who didn't come back from the Alamo. As we rode along, I had nothing to do but think. I wondered out loud who would help them now, mentioning the names of our friends, individually. Nita and Mama were thinking the same things, wondering about our friends.

"Everyone is okay, Sydnie. You rest," Nita said.

But I knew that no one was okay.

Our wagon lurched to a sudden stop. Someone came to ask who was riding with us. Friends of Mary Milsaps were concerned for her and her seven children. Mary was blind, and her husband had been at the Alamo. Houston organized a search party wanting to ensure that she was led out of the territory and carried to safety.

The soldiers were looking thoroughly for her, wagon by wagon. We watched the soldiers as far as we could see, but it didn't appear that anyone gave them any information.

The day wore on, and we pressed toward the Colorado River. The rain was relentless. We made very slow progress.

At the end of the first day, the night turned black as pitch. The darkness was welcomed. We wanted to be invisible. We didn't stop the wagons until the drivers couldn't see their way. We had made only about ten miles. Somewhere on the prairie, we came upon more than twenty wagons and we camped with them. Our sense of security increased with the additional number of campers.

Every farm, every settlement, every campsite was to be evacuated from San Antonio to Louisiana. The roadway was quickly filling with refugees.

We didn't dare make a fire the first night, for fear of becoming known to Mexican spies scouting for Santa Anna. Daddy got out and talked quietly with some of the other men. After a while, word came that we'd be camping here until daylight. The women got out and combined their food. We had cornbread wrapped in a flour sack and a pot of cold beans. In order to avoid the typical clanging of a camp, we ate with our hands, just breaking the bread and scooping the beans with fingers. We all crept and whispered, knowing our lives depended on our concealment. Without ceremony, we ate what was passed to us in the darkness, licked our fingers, and faced the night. It was eerily quiet, and I remembered my brother.

When Nita passed my cornbread, I shared the inevitable news—the signs of childbirth were beginning. It was time to devise a plan for the arrival of the Kellogg baby.

Nita told my mother and Ma Kellogg that I needed help. The women slipped back into the wagon with me and stealthily moved all the bundles around to the sides. They put one quilt down and saved the others to be clean for later. I knew that silence was important, and I couldn't betray us. I took off my heavy cotton stockings and rolled one into a ball. I clenched the rolled stocking between my teeth to choke back my cries of pain as the long night wore on. The older women in my family kept a basin nearby to wash my face with the other stocking dipped into the icy rain water. It was a night of agony, and daylight arrived before the baby.

As the wagon train began to roll the next morning, the motion of our wagon made me feel better. My labor had eased some, and the rocking of the wagon must have encouraged the infant to find his path. Late in the morning, my mother informed my daddy that he would be stopping for the event. Our wagon pulled out of the caravan, and some of the others pulled out with us. As nature took her course, a tiny baby boy appeared in the wagon.

Two women kindled a fire in a huge cooking pot as two others tied a large piece of oil cloth between the wagons to keep the rain off us. A tin ladle of water was held over the small fire, just long enough to see it sizzle. A knife was sterilized by placing the blade in the blaze of the flames, and the cord connecting me to my baby was severed. Mama took the child, and soon I heard a whimper. The woman used the hot water sparingly to clean me up. They changed the quilt, wrapped the baby in blankets, and washed away the waste with cold water. In a short time, the whimper became a series of loud, short cries. I was a mother again.

March 16, 1836 – Mina and the Woman from the Woods

On the edge of a grassy prairie, tucked under a clump of oaks, our band of twenty-eight women with their forty-nine children rose silently to begin the third day of our journey. Six men circulated among us offering help. The wagons were filled to capacity. Daddy and Papa Kellogg put six children with their mothers on the benches of our wagons. The men would walk, leading the mules by their reins. The smallest children were packed on the backs of mules and horses, in between bundles hanging at their sides. The older children carried what they could beside them. Skids made of tree limbs were dragged behind the wagons, loaded with as much as could be tied on.

The names of our friends and neighbors came to mind. As best we could learn, everyone was accounted for except Mary Milsaps and her children.

On that morning, we began to realize it would be difficult to salvage everything we wanted. A feather bed was still on the ground where four children spent a sleepless night with their mother. A wolf pack howled in the dark and scared the wits out of the entire little family. In their haste to move closer into the camp, the worn canvas snagged on a briar and feathers were littering the ground. Their mother was instructing them to fold the canvas and bring it, as they might stuff it with field grass and still have their bed.

The little ones moaned, and their mothers tried to console them. The children were hungry. A quick apple or a piece of leather jerky would have to do for breakfast that morning. The widows would have no coffee. Hunger would take second place to fear. Our fear of Santa Anna drove us on early that morning. We wouldn't dally until we reached the Colorado River.

With everyone eager to go, we began our third day. It continued much like the first two—cold, wet, and miserable. We knew only our relentless desperation to escape what we had known as home, turning to what we knew as hope for our children. Our only choice was to move on.

More families appeared along the way, merging into the wagon train as they could. I counted twenty wagons at one point, but that was just as far as I could see. There were more beyond the horizon in both directions.

The escape out of Gonzales was much like our journey into Tejas, with travelers helping each other and being on guard for the safety of everyone. The families from Gonzales stayed together for the benefit of the widows. We were hoping to assist each other, not only in our escape, but also in the eventual return to rebuild our town. The logical route was from river to river, making our way east from one river to the next. We'd go to the Colorado first, then to the Brazos, then to the Trinity and Little Bayou just east of Harrisburg. If we could cross the Sabine, we would be safe.

Sam Houston was at least a day ahead of us. We could tell we were catching up by what lingered in his wake. There were grumblers, hesitant deserters—men who wouldn't keep their oath of loyalty to Sam Houston's army but couldn't completely let go of their ambition to be a part of a republic if it came. Hundreds left the volunteer ranks to go back to other settlements and rescue their families. Others just hung back.

Many had fallen away from the main force but hadn't really abandoned the trail. We could see them, camped in the distance. Some came to walk along with us for a while. They wanted Houston to stand against the Mexicans, but not so much that they would stand with Houston.

We had plenty of drinking water from all the rain. But some days passed without a meal. Just as the tree line to the west began to hide the sun, we found ourselves in the community of travelers who had gotten to Mina before us. It was the first ferry crossing on the Colorado. We'd have a much-needed rest.

What a pitiful community it was. We were a caravan of dirty, hungry, sickly women still in shock, with children needing all kinds of help. Some women were just awakening to the emotional devastation delivered days before. Some cried out and fell down on the ground. Some beat themselves and screamed. Some just looked at their children with desperate eyes. Papa Kellogg and

Daddy helped as much as they could, but there were many needs the men couldn't fill.

God placed an angel among the desperate refugees at Mina. A woman who called herself Sal appeared among the Gonzales wagons soon after we arrived. She looked for women to help. For that there was no shortage.

The woman was robust and strong. She was filthy and barefoot, having no more comfort than those she helped. Sal was the face of love with the touch of life. It started with the first desperate woman on the road. Sal lifted the crying woman and carried her to a little knoll by a campfire. The full-bodied woman brought a tin of coffee and wrapped the widow's hands around the warm cup. Squatting beside the distraught woman, she used her own massive skirt to wipe the tears away from a tortured face. Without words, the saintly woman wrapped a soiled but soft crocheted shawl around the trembling shoulders of the frail one, who seemed to gain her composure enough to have a sip of the hot liquid. Then Sal disappeared into the crowd, appearing from time to time to assist other women who couldn't seem to help themselves.

It was an amazing thing to see the terrors melt away with a brief application of human kindness.

I never knew where she came from. Some said she lived in the Mina area and was determined to stay in her home. Others said she refused to give in to Santa Anna's threats. She was a mystical presence for our stay at the river crossing, and I would never see her again after we left.

It was here the Methodist circuit minister caught up with the crowds. He went from camp to camp praying with us. He touched the children on their heads and simply closed his eyes in prayer. Tears ran down his dusty cheeks. He intended to be a source of strength, but his heart was broken.

"Bless you as you go," he whispered. "May God be with you," he offered as he walked away and on to the next pitiful soul.

He longed for something to encourage us, but he seemed overwhelmed with the sadness of the sight. All he could offer was the hope of his prayers, and we were grateful for that.

The river was raging beyond her banks. The ferry was a strong contraption, with pull ropes. It carried two wagons on each crossing, and as many people as could be loaded without sinking her. It would be at least another day before our turn would come. Word spread, and everyone from Gonzales made a temporary camp. The women loosened the harnesses and corralled the animals. Nita took the tiny baby while Mama K and Mama tied quilts between our wagons to make a shelter. I was able to make my first excursion outside the wagon since the first night.

As I crawled toward the back flap of our wagon, my head was spinning. I felt like sharp stones were grinding against the tissue inside my belly. Bodily fluids came up and out. The quilt was rancid, and the smell followed me. As I dragged myself along on my elbows, a bloody mass appeared behind me in a trail on the quilt. A dark spirit overcame me then. I fell out of the wagon and tumbled to the ground. I imagined falling into a hole and pulling a crust of earth over me. I wanted to be free of the pain in my gut. I wanted to be clean and safe again.

There on the ground next to the wagon wheel, I pushed leaves and mud away in a pile, making a hole in the earth. I relieved myself as much as possible. I remembered a barn cat back in Kentucky, thinking now how we were reduced to living like the animals.

Nita came to help me and realized what I was trying to accomplish. She pulled the soiled quilt out of the wagon and folded it so the cleaner corners were on the outside. Together we made a bed as dry as possible, knowing we would leave it all behind when we left.

My beloved robe was already ruined with the fluids of childbirth, so we sacrificed it as another layer over the ground. I stretched out and tensed my muscles as best I could. Walking wasn't possible, but I could crawl and stretch. Sleeping on the ground while I had the chance was better than staying in the wagon another night. I leaned against the wagon wheel and waited for my head to stop spinning.

John Benjamin's mother had been quiet since the horrible news came to us in Gonzales. Caring for her new grandson gave her some comfort. She came to me with the child and laid him across my lap, explaining how she was feeding him with natural food—a mixture of our food and a bit of milk donated from a milk cow someone brought along. She said he was a tough one like his dad, that he was quiet and a good traveler. I was skeptical. I'd been through this before.

As young John Benjamin lay across my body, his little thumb between slender lips, I knew I could not care for him now. Whatever was afflicting my body would be spread through any milk I'd give him, and his life would be threatened. I looked at Johnny's mother. I was blessed to have this woman who was so wise. Her face was gaunt. Her eyes were sunken, her lips were a pale purple with dry bits of skin peeling away. Her fingers were cold. Her hands were shaking as she struggled to position the baby. Icy streams of rain water dripped from the strands of hair sticking out from the bandana wrapped around her head.

Mama Kellogg did have some joyful news, however. "Mary Milsaps was found with all of her children. They were hiding in the underbrush near their home. Praise God, something to be thankful for," she said.

The search party brought the Milsaps to the Gonzales wagons so they could be carried across the river with the rest of us. This news warmed our hearts and gave us a sense of victory. The rescue of Mary Milsaps bolstered our courage.

Ma Kellogg went about doing what had to be done, ignoring the tears trickling silently from her eyes. I knew my baby was the child who would fill the jagged hole Santa Anna had torn in her heart.

"Let this boy sleep here for a while," she said. "I'll be back for him later." And she was gone again.

The precious child slept, as if he knew he was among desperate folks with little comfort to offer. I marveled at how he could rest so peacefully so near to death and chaos. I wondered if he would need a tiny carved casket before he would get back to Gonzales, but quickly forced the thought from my head. No, he was strong, and his eyes were full of life. He and little Eugene seemed to be the strongest among us just now. It seemed a miracle that Mama Kellogg could take such good care of my baby. I prayed motherhood would resume for me when I was healthy again.

"Here's some stew, Syd. Try it."

Nita handed me a tin filled with a thick broth and heavy chunks of squirrel meat. She took my son so I could eat. It was delicious at first but didn't stay down long. I wiped my face on the skirt of my robe and drank some water.

"He looks like John Benjamin," she said.

She cuddled the baby and I was overcome with gratitude for my friend and my family.

"He is John Benjamin," I said with as much of a smile as I could manage.

Folks had been camping in Mina for several days before we arrived, awaiting the river crossing. There was food and a warm fire. It reminded me of what Gonzales had been when we first arrived there only five years ago. There were men to help the widows. They were busy attending to wagon repairs, knowing the long trip we would face on the other side of the river.

I dozed throughout the night. In my sleep I met the monsters. Whether from the delirium of my infections and high fever or from the dark reality of our plight, I don't know. At Mina, the devils began to visit my sleep. They were faithful companions through to the end.

March 20, 1836 – Horse Thieves at Beeson's Landing

The noise of the caravan began before first light, and we resumed our flight to safety. The wagons moved forward, and the ferry was pulled across the flood waters. Everyone who wanted to cross was delivered to the east bank of the Colorado River. The Methodist circuit preacher came on the last ferry. They pulled the flat barge up against the landing on the east bank and took hatchets to it. The ferry was broken apart, and the pull ropes taken down. Nothing was useful any more. Sal, who had comforted so many, stood on the west bank of the river at the remains of the demolished ferry landing. Her silhouette grew smaller as we left her there to endure whatever the Mexican Army would bring.

For the next two days, we crept along through the Colorado River Valley. The west bank was a high, sharp drop from above. But along the east bank, most of the land was a gradual, sloshing, shallow flood across a wide sand bar.

"This side is wide, flat land and low. We'll know who's on the other side long before they can reach us," Pop Kellogg said.

The water came in waves against the stretch of sand. We guided the wagons up to the road a ways off from the river's edge.

We were more exhausted and less panicked, and our pace slowed a bit. The muddy ruts in the well-worn road buried the wagon wheels almost to the axles. Mud was thrown outward, and those who walked kept their distance from the road to avoid the sludge. Our path was wide and long, our pace slow but deliberate.

During the second day on the east bank, we were approached by a man on horseback. He was alone. He fell in step with a woman leading a single horse on the edge of our wagon train, some distance from the others. She was loaded down with her children and her baggage. The man was a land pirate, bent on scavenging what

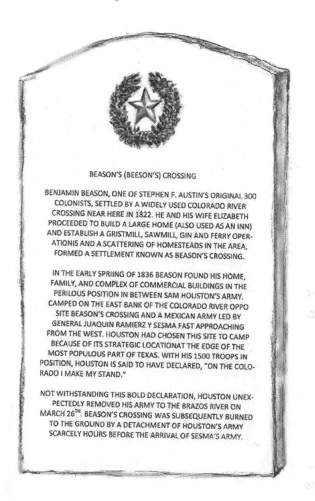

BEASON'S (BEESON'S) CROSSING

BENJAMIN BEASON, ONE OF STEPHEN F. AUSTIN'S ORIGINAL 300 COLONISTS, SETTLED BY A WIDELY USED COLORADO RIVER CROSSING NEAR HERE IN 1822. HE AND HIS WIFE ELIZABETH PROCEEDED TO BUILD A LARGE HOME (ALSO USED AS AN INN) AND ESTABLISH A GRISTMILL, SAWMILL, GIN AND FERRY OPER-ATIONIS AND A SCATTERING OF HOMESTEADS IN THE AREA, FORMED A SETTLEMENT KNOWN AS BEASON'S CROSSING.

IN THE EARLY SPRIING OF 1836 BEASON FOUND HIS HOME, FAMILY, AND COMPLEX OF COMMERCIAL BUILDINGS IN THE PERILOUS POSITION IN BETWEEN SAM HOUSTON'S ARMY. CAMPED ON THE EAST BANK OF THE COLORADO RIVER OPPO SITE BEASON'S CROSSING AND A MEXICAN ARMY LED BY GENERAL JUAQUIN RAMIERZ Y SESMA FAST APPROACHING FROM THE WEST. HOUSTON HAD CHOSEN THIS SITE TO CAMP BECAUSE OF ITS STRATEGIC LOCATIONAT THE EDGE OF THE MOST POPULOUS PART OF TEXAS. WITH HIS 1500 TROOPS IN POSITION, HOUSTON IS SAID TO HAVE DECLARED, "ON THE COLO-RADO I MAKE MY STAND."

NOT WITHSTANDING THIS BOLD DECLARATION, HOUSTON UNEX-PECTEDLY REMOVED HIS ARMY TO THE BRAZOS RIVER ON MARCH 26TH. BEASON'S CROSSING WAS SUBSEQUENTLY BURNED TO THE GROUND BY A DETACHMENT OF HOUSTON'S ARMY SCARCELY HOURS BEFORE THE ARRIVAL OF SESMA'S ARMY.

Beeson's Crossing

meager bounty he might get. He was the worst kind of opportun-ist, taking advantage of the helpless where he could find them.

"I need that horse," the man said. "General Houston, he needs as many horses as we can bring in." He got off his horse and began removing the children from their mount.

Papa Kellogg started towards the conflict, about six wag-ons away, and off some distance into the prairie. Mac pulled his buckboard in that direction, heading toward the assaulted family. The woman stumbled to the ground. Two little girls ran in fear, and the little boy kicked the man's leg.

The woman stood and began to curse him. "If Sam Houston needs this horse, he can come tell me himself," she said.

Before Papa and Mac arrived, there were seven women tearing into the man, all screaming, kicking, and fighting him for all they were worth. One woman held the reins of his agitated horse.

"Get back on this horse and ride, you son of a billy goat!" the woman shouted at him.

One woman beat him with a branch she picked up off the ground. Another woman used a buggy whip on him. They dragged him to the ground and kicked him, whereupon he put his arms over his head and pulled his legs up under him.

Papa Kellogg was never much of a fighter, but his presence seemed to change the attitude of the horse thief. Then Mac arrived on the scene. He exchanged some words, handed the man his hat, and gestured to his horse. Papa never had to raise a hand. The man uncurled himself and got to his feet. He stood like a coward, looking at Papa and Mac, surveying the women. He backed away without words, with a look of vengeance on his face. He took the reins of his horse, mounted up, and looked down at the frail women who had beaten him. Then he disappeared into the horizon.

The woman under assault gathered her frightened children. Her friends helped her repack the coveted horse, and the caravan continued.

Now the grumbling against Sam Houston became louder and more widespread. All of us resented him for his apparent cowardice.

"Gonzales gave all we had, and Houston runs away."

It seemed to us that Houston should take a stand against the Mexican Army, in the same way we had refused to give up the cannon last October.

Running away and being assaulted on the road didn't make any sense but we would have to live to sort it out. Living required running. For now we would run.

The terrain beyond the edge of the river was a grassy plain. We made good time traveling there. We caught up with the army at their camp near Columbus at Beeson's Landing. We passed the army camp, went about a half mile further, and stopped for the night. He might have been a coward, but we felt safer with Houston and all his men between us and the Mexican Army.

The west bank at Beeson's Landing was high and steep with a dredge cut for the ferry. But the east bank was a broad, flat plain rising gently from the river. The ferry was on the east side, and we would know about any troops coming from the west long before they could reach us.

Mr. Beeson did all he could to make us as comfortable as possible for our brief stay. The old man visited our camp and spoke from his horse, giving encouragement where he could.

"My home is yours for this brief time. When you leave, the ferry and all the buildings will be burned," he told us. "Nothing I have will give comfort to our common enemy. Your loss is felt here on the Colorado. Beeson is your Texian brother."

Our rest at Beeson's Landing was a turning point for us. Houston drilled his men, and they began to look like a real army. They stood in straight lines and marched in formation. General Houston rode his white horse in front of them, and when he gave an order the men responded like real soldiers.

"Well, finally there is some organization about them," one woman said to my mother. "Maybe Houston knows what he's doing after all."

Realizing the cohesiveness of the men under Houston, we felt a new resolve to live and see our home again. While there was no joy in the camp, a sense of hope crept in among us. In fact we felt so secure in the presence of Houston's army we decided to stay at our Beeson camp for a second night.

As a full moon shown down on more than fifty wagons camped beyond the east bank of the Colorado River, two unshaven and unkind men sat on horses in a distant, low clump of brush. They were following us, determined to take what one of them had not been able to take a few days before. They waited a long while until the moon was high, feeling sure that we had given in to our exhaustion for the night. Like hungry wolves, they crept into our camp. With the stealth of experienced thieves, they each loosed the reins of a single horse.

We had circled the wagons and corralled the horses in the center of the camp to avoid losing them. Several widows were posted as guards, and they sat in the shadows. They were so small and still they were invisible to the intruders. They each held a single-shot long rifle.

As the two men took their first fleeing steps, one of the women raised her weapon in the shadows and took a well-placed shot. No one saw her. Only the explosion from the barrel echoed across the camp as the first man fell dead. Another shot dropped the second man, and the two horses bolted. The camp was in complete turmoil until we understood what was happening. Daddy and Pop Kellogg drug the bodies out into the far field, where they left them for the vultures.

Early the next morning, a scouting team of women went to fetch the runaway horses. They came back with four animals. The two mounts belonging to the thieves became part of our herd, and six more children rode on newly acquired saddles.

In short order we broke camp and formed a line that would move eastward to the Brazos. Looking back from our wagon train, we could see the smoke we knew was the last of the Beeson place. Our small victories were bittersweet. I wondered what awaited us ahead.

March 24, 1836 – Burying a Child, the Art of Fire, and a Newspaper in San Felipe

The first day out from Beeson's was just another shade of chilling gray. The terrain reminded me of the Gulf when we left New Orleans. Flooded fields were transformed by pockets of shallow waves. I noticed an object floating in a little pond not too far from the trail. It looked to be the same doll I had seen in the store the last day I worked there, waiting for Nita and Grace. I pointed to it, calling it to Nita's attention. She had seen the doll at the store and thought as I did that it should be saved. She thought she'd go retrieve it, as she was nimble enough to dash out to it and be back before the wagons were much farther along. My dear, agile friend slid over the back of the wagon and out between the flaps of canvas.

I smiled, thinking of my little son. The thought of returning this treasure to its owner gave me some pleasure, and I was thinking ahead to a day I'd make a doll for my little John Benjamin.

Then I heard Nita scream.

I thought she'd encountered a snake. The wagon jolted to a stop. The screaming continued. In seconds, Nita was back to our caravan holding her hands over her face. Pop Kellogg came down off his seat and went to the place where Nita had been. He bent down and picked up what wasn't a doll at all.

We had come upon a dead child. Maybe she fell and drowned. Or maybe the child died from a disease, and her body was left behind. Maybe the child's mother was distracted and didn't yet know the child was missing. Life had been gone from the little body for some time already. She was rigid. The wagons ahead of the Gonzales group had moved on. There was no way to know how far ahead her mother rode, or where her family was now. But Pop Kellogg and Daddy would not go on until they buried the poor child.

We pulled out of the wagon train, and Daddy got his shovel. He cut a piece out of our quilt and brought the frigid baby body to my mama.

"Rebecca, take that little dress off her and wrap her in this quilt. We'll need that dress to identify this baby to her mother if we can ever find her."

Then the two grandfathers took the little one out into the field. Daddy carried her gently as if she might awaken if he moved too suddenly. They walked until they reached the highest place. Hugging my own warm little baby, I watched from the distance, thinking how impossible the scene was.

They knelt out there and bowed their heads. They cut into the ground, digging and laying the mud in a mound beside them. It seemed the world was standing still, and the two men on the rise moved in slow motion. They refilled the hole and stood up. Slowly, reluctantly, they left her there and walked slowly back down from the hill.

I heard their heavy breathing and coughing, but they weren't talking. Pop Kellogg went back to his own wagon. Daddy stood and wiped his face on the back of his arm. He took out a handkerchief from his back pocket and blew his nose. Daddy knelt down on one knee, just being quiet for a moment. He turned his face to the sky and seemed to be looking for some assurance that what he had done was acceptable.

"Let's move on," he said as he climbed up to the seat of the wagon. "Our next stop is San Felipe. Ho, Barley. Get up, there."

With a snap of the long leather reins, we were off again.

Since we'd stayed at Beeson's an extra night, we wanted to make up time. The rain was hard early in the day but slackened in the late afternoon. The terrain was flat, and the moon was bright enough to travel through the night. We kept going until we reached the Brazos River Valley.

"This was the first community of settlers Austin started," Papa explained to Mama. "It's a gracious little town. Some good men were here for our meeting back in the fall. Whoa, Barley. Hold up there."

The wagon train came to a stop. It was deep into night. Just before we reached the town, a woman came around to tell us, "Camp here tonight. Tomorrow we'll pass over the Brazos."

Everyone got out of the wagons to have our supper and bed down. We had gone through the same routine so many times by now most of the evening preparations were routine. Building a fire during this wet, cold season was a challenge, but Ma Kellogg had it down to an art form.

"Here's your tinderbox." Pop Kellogg tossed my mother-in-law a little leather pouch with the things she needed to make our campfire. "I'll unharness these animals."

Everyone had a job, and we didn't need to discuss it anymore. While Daddy and Papa Kellogg settled the animals, Mama organized flat, dry stones into a firepit. Dry kindling was laid on. Ma Kellogg had four sharp pokers. Mama loaded them with potatoes, onions, and whatever meat we had caught during the day. We had a variety of crawfish and frog legs. Some days we had squirrel. If someone up the trail got a deer, they shared meat as far as it would go. Whatever was to be cooked on the fire went on the pokers first. Mama took out a great skillet, and the pokers fit perfectly within that skillet.

Then came the art. Ma Kellogg took out her leather pouch. With what looked like secrecy, she removed a twist of threads which contained a bit of gunpowder. She laid the cord of threads across the kindling, and she pulled out a knife and a small stone. Then the magic began. As skilled as a surgeon, she rubbed the blade across the stone, touching the threads exactly the right way. As she drew the blade back, a spark snapped into the cloth. The gunpowder puffed into a tiny flame. Mama K cupped her hands and gently blew life into the infant flames. With a long, steady, quiet breath, the flames licked into the kindling, and soon we had a proper campfire. The stones heated, the skillet got hot, the bits of food on the poker sizzled, and the family prepared to eat our supper.

Sharing a fire bonded us on the trail just as it had at the town square when we first arrived in Gonzales. Words could not express the depth of loss we all felt, but sharing the evening fire connected us in our common plight. The scene of the camp each night became sadly beautiful. I saw it as a tiny glow of hope burning for each family. That night Mac brought his wagon near ours, and Nita stayed with him the rest of the journey. We broke camp the next morning and headed through the little town of San Felipe on our way to the ferry on the Brazos River.

"My lord, George, look at that." Mama pointed to a row of notices posted on the wall of the general store in the town of San Felipe.

THE REPUBLIC OF TEXAS was boldly printed on the notices.

"How can they say that, George?"

"It's politics, my dear." He patted her knee. "We can only hope it works out that way. This town gets all the news, and they can print what they want cause they have that newspaper." He motioned to a slender building between the general store and a saloon. "They held that convention here and that's what they voted, but now we just have to see how things go."

We crossed the Brazos on a ferry, just like we did in Mina. As we made our way east, illness spread. Not all the food we ate stayed down. The children cried. The women coughed. At night, some awakened screaming in panic. Many mornings we discovered the lifeless bodies of friends who just gave up in the night. Daddy and Pop Kellogg did the burying and did it as respectfully as they could.

We buried more children along the way, and those remaining alive became skeletal. Cholera, whooping cough, dysentery, measles, open wounds with infection, insect bites, and sores packed with mud on our feet were all widespread conditions. Skin, hair, teeth, and eyes were all subjected to the filth of neglect and the misfortune of exposure. Our hands carried disease to everything we touched. But the little boy to whom I had given birth remained unaffected. My promise to his father was coming true. He would live, and he would make his family proud.

My fever spiked every night, and I shivered all day. My ears rang, my eyes blurred, and my thoughts were often foggy. As I drifted in and out of consciousness, the monsters visited me. I was aware and somewhat ashamed of the luxury I had to ride in our own wagon, as so many had to walk.

Our strongest motivation was the children. Their future was an unwritten story, none of us knowing what was in store for them. But we knew they would have to be alive to have any future and to inherit anything from the struggles of their parents. The widows had been strong pioneer women in partnership with ambitious men who were now all gone. We survived by the hour, not knowing what the next moment held in store. But very soon we would take our rest.

April 18, 1836 – Crossing the Sabine at Hickman's Ferry

We arrived in Louisiana on April eighteenth. We crossed the Sabine River at Hickman's Ferry, a good, hard ground where cattle crossed for many years. President Jackson already had troops stationed there. We discovered a little village of Army tents with campfires and strong men ready to help us.

The soldiers of the United States formed a receiving line of sorts, just on the Louisiana side of the marshes that composed the

Sabine River bottom. The shock on the faces of the men who received us reflected our miserable state. They stared at us in disbelief and reached out hands of mercy. We were so tired, and we moved very slowly. They received us gently and encouraged us to rest.

Everyone on the wagon train had triumphed beyond our physical capacity and had risen above excruciating burdens. As we passed among the soldiers, they were deeply moved. We had outrun a devil and were now treated with long-overdue tenderness. The soldiers respected the ragged remains of decimated women with their helpless children accompanied by a few haggard, broken-down men.

The soldiers were particularly concerned with the plight of the children. Here were the youngest pioneers, sacrificing their youth, and reduced to human salvage. Perhaps they thought of their own dear ones left at home or remembered their own childhood. Whatever the connection, the tie was obvious as the soldiers lingered in their care of the youngsters.

"You folks take your children over to those tents. Our men will help you. Just sit down, ma'am, here on these blankets. I'll bring you water, and you can wash," the soldiers told us.

As I sat in a shelter, I saw a frail boy walking aimlessly with his smaller sister. The boy had an infected eye. He brushed flies away with his free hand but held fast to his sister with the other. She was sobbing softly, and her nose was running. Leaves and twigs were tangled in the clumps of her hair. Their clothes were threadbare, now thoroughly filthy. They appeared to be dressed only in mud. And they were lost from their mother.

A young soldier went to them and lifted one in each of his strong arms. As he turned, I saw anguish on his handsome face and the look of complete dismay in his eyes. He wouldn't be separated from them. He took them to a wash pot and sat them down. He wiped their dirty faces with a clean cloth. When he offered the girl his handkerchief, she reached out to him. He took her in his arms and hugged her as if she was his own.

The children looked at the young man longingly, and it appeared he would take responsibility for them. My attention was then drawn to others in small pockets of the camp, noticing the compassionate efforts of all the soldiers.

Everyone from the wagon train was afflicted with multiple diseases, and my infections had gotten worse. It was impossible to know which or how many illnesses anyone had. It didn't matter because we had so little medical care. Once we camped on the east side of the Sabine, my illness raged. My body shook, my head went dizzy, and my insides spewed contaminated body fluids. My breathing was stifled. My skin itched from filth and disease. But as bad as it was, I was the fortunate one. I had ridden, while many had walked. I had family, but many others had no family to help them.

As the first evening settled in, we smelled the aroma of cabbage, ham, and biscuits. We thought we had crossed into heaven. But heaven was yet to come.

April 23, 1836 – Unfinished Business

"Johnson, let's have some of that guitar over here." A man lumbered over to join the harmonica player. Music had been flowing across the camp for a half hour.

Rest was never so good as it was for the refugees on the banks of the Sabine. Armies are meant for conquests, but Jackson's army was restoring us. They made a little village in the woods with shelters of blankets tied between our wagons. We sat for long periods of time, resting and waiting.

"What are you thinking, daughter?" Daddy sat down next to me with army coffee in his own tin cup. Evening was falling, and we had a little campfire.

"I've been thinking, Daddy. I'm remembering John Benjamin and my brother."

He nodded his head and looked at my mama sitting across from him in a small family circle. We had nothing to do now but sit and remember. Eugene yawned and lay down on Mama's lap. Ma Kellogg looked at my little baby in her arms.

"John Benjamin the Third," she said. "This child made it this far. He's blessed with strength."

Pa Kellogg pulled the little blanket away from the child's eyes and gently touched his little nose. "He's gonna be just fine." He nodded his head, "Outa this misery will come something good. We just have to all keep strong." He lay down and put his hat over his face for a nap.

The campfire crackled, and flashes of the light reflected in Daddy's eyes. I remembered the sandhill cranes and their loyalty to the flock. My thoughts went back to Gonzales. "Daddy, I need to tell you something important."

"I'm listening."

"It's about C.J. over at the blacksmith shop."

He took a sip of his coffee, nodded his head, and waited.

"John told me something about C.J., and we need to write a letter …" I was struggling for my breath, and it was hard for me to continue.

"Sydna, I think I know what you're trying to tell me. Your brother and I had a good talk. It was after John Benjamin came back from his time with Burleson in San Antonio. Our boy got worried, like he knew something was going to happen to him. He told me C.J. was a Schmidt, and he wanted the other brothers to know."

I felt relieved and relaxed a bit. Daddy smiled a sad smile and got that serious faraway look on his face. It was the same look I saw on the day he first told us of the possibility of war. It was a determined look that acknowledged the high and painful price of something worth having.

"Don't you worry, girl. We already sent a letter to Edgar in New Orleans. He should have it by now. You just rest."

"Where is C.J., Daddy? Did he go to San Antonio?"

"I don't know." He looked around the camp. "I haven't seen Juanita or C.J. since we left Gonzales. Folks have gone in every direction. Things happen. People get lost in times like these. I don't know where he went, but his brothers will know he is a good man, wherever he is."

I closed my eyes and went to sleep.

April 25, 1836 – Texas Is Free

On the afternoon of April twenty-fifth, two men came riding into camp waving their hats and stirring up the dust. They were yelling, getting everyone's attention. My burning head told me it was a warning to run again, away from the Mexican Army. I thought, *Just leave me here to die. I can't run anymore.*

But no!

"Texas is free!" they yelled. "Old Sam defeated the Mexican Army. Santa Anna is a prisoner. Texas declared independence from Mexico. You can go back home now!"

We could hardly believe it. The news came with a painful sting. It should have been another victory for my brother and my husband, but they were part of the price.

Going home—but it was all burned up. I began to imagine going back to Gonzales on that long road we had just traveled.

In my head, I understood what had been accomplished, but I didn't feel it in my heart. No one in the Davis-Kellogg camp shouted for joy. I noticed most of the women and children stood quietly in the emptiness of the announcement.

That evening the Kelloggs and the Davises had a family meeting. Mama and Daddy were eager to make a new life in what was left of Gonzales.

The Kelloggs were less inclined to go that far. They believed their best choice was to make their way slowly. They planned to find lodging around Harrisburg and then visit family in the northern regions.

"Last I heard from my sister, she was living on a place called Parker Fort. I think it's not so far from here." Ma Kellogg looked at Papa.

"We'll take our time and go that direction," Pa said. "I think some others are headed that way. We'll get back to Gonzales later in the year."

I was in no condition to even have a conversation about it. The elders of my family made a plan for my son to travel back to Gonzales with the Davises, to be his father's legacy. I would stay a while in Harrisburg with the Kelloggs until my health was better.

I watched as the Gonzales widows found the determination to pack and redesign their futures. Mac and Nita were among the first to go. When Nita came to say goodbye, I lied to her. I drew on my last fragment of courage to make her believe I could start again.

"I love you dearly, my friend," I said as we shared a long, warm hug. "The miles will seem shorter going home. We'll build another tavern and call it Miller's again."

She smiled at me and held my cold hands.

"I'll come there as soon as I can. You can watch for me from up in the attic." I tried to laugh.

I knew the Sabine was a turning point for everyone who made it there. Not one of us would ever be the same, and I doubted I would ever make it back to Gonzales.

May 1, 1836 – Death in Harrisburg

Harrisburg. Surely I could make it that far. Hopefully we'd get medical help there. The men who told us we could go back to Texas recommended Harrisburg because it was the temporary capital of the new republic. The trip would be a fraction of the distance to Gonzales. The Davises and the Kelloggs would go as far as Harrisburg together.

Two wagons carrying our family traveled along the north edge of Trinity Bay, heading due west. We arrived in Harrisburg on the evening of May first. My first glimpse of the waste of Harrisburg soured in my stomach. My hope for some level of civilization was crushed under the wagon wheels as they rolled across the charred ruins left behind by the Mexican army. The wagons stopped.

The last orange rays of sun straining to come in from the west lit up a flag that hung from a large tent dead ahead of us. There was an emblem with the painted form of a woman, her clothes partially torn away leaving her chest bare. She held out a sword. Across the sword was a banner with some words. My eyes riveted on the words LIBERTY and DEATH written boldly on the pennant draped across her sword.

It was then I knew Harrisburg was speaking to me, and the two words on the banner were my destiny. On that flag before me was the image of a woman exposed and vulnerable, yet defiant. For that woman liberty and death were inseparable. I was that woman.

The men of our family repacked the wagons, and we exchanged lingering, tight hugs. We looked deeply into each other's eyes and whispered a temporary farewell, promising to meet again. The lie I repeated was deepening my despair. I took a long, soulful look at my infant son, wanting to see his father's eyes. I kissed his little hands, knowing they would complete his father's work. For the first time since it all happened, I allowed myself to cry over the

San Jacinto Battle Flag

deep despondent sadness of the insurmountable loss of Gonzales. Then my mother took my baby.

As the infant left my arms, I knew he was my legacy of family love. For all my life, all I wanted was to share the love of family I had known from my beginning. The whole town of Gonzales became our family, where love was extended to an orphan and to a girl wronged by Indians. I remembered the love shown by the woman from the woods to the family of desperate souls in Mina. Even the battle-hardened men of Jackson's army could not suppress their sense of human love for the little ones at the Sabine. If the celebration of human love was my goal, I had accomplished that. Now, our baby, John Benjamin, would bring that love full circle back to Gonzales.

The Davises headed southwest for Gonzales. I watched as their wagon grew smaller, and something terminal possessed me. In the open, flat ranges of the Gulf Coast prairie grass, the lives that would bring Texas's future down in DeWitt County moved on with what grit they still possessed. But I had nothing left.

Pop made a camp. Elizabeth Kellogg, my son's grandmother, stayed by my side. They laid me on the ground atop quilts that emitted the aromas of our recent adventure. I could smell it all—the salty air of the great Gulf, the stench of the Indian boy's dog, the sweat of vulgar men, and roasting frog legs. I saw Mariah's scars and Jessie's owl eyes. All at once, and yet individually, the scenes played out across the back of my eyelids. I saw mud dripping over a cannon barrel, and the chill of frozen rain embraced me.

I tried to explain it to her, but Johnny's mother just kept trying to give me some water. My tongue was sticking to the roof of my mouth. I couldn't see her face, and my ears were ringing. I heard unrecognizable voices.

As I tried to identify those around me, I once again heard birds singing. The breath I took in became more unwilling. My hands flailed as I gasped for reluctant breaths. Finally my arms grew too heavy to lift. Letting the hallucination of that moment take its own course, I found myself transported to a little hill near the Carter place where John Benjamin and I went for a picnic. In my mind I looked up directly into the Texas sky and saw a tunnel of light leading up to the sun. My hands warmed, and I felt strong enough to sit up. And when I did, I saw John Gaston. The brother with whom I'd played and traveled and worked to come so far was there reaching out to me.

"Come on, Sydna," he said. "Let's go home."

As I reached up, my spirit slipped away. The devastated body of Sydnie Gaston Kellogg remained on the ground. Ascending, I looked back to see the expanse of what was now the Republic of Texas spread out below us. She was green and lush, with veins of blue rivers promising new life. We arose in the late spring sunshine. Just beyond the clouds, John Benjamin took my hand. I felt complete. Our work would live on long after us, and the generations to come would be glad.

Epilogue

Throughout the years since the Battle of Gonzales, the loss of the Alamo, and the Runaway Scrape, many questions about the people involved remain unanswered. Too many facts were left in the ashes. But we should not let that darkness eclipse the light of the wonderful people who did so much for us.

Sydnie Gaston Miller Kellogg was my great, great, great grandmother. The baby born to her on the Runaway Scrape lived to continue the Kellogg family line. I remember my father reminiscing about his grandfather, William Crockett, who was Sydnie's grandson.

The unanswered questions will never be fully resolved. We can know only what is documented. This story uses islands of truth connected by bridges of logic to weave together a fictional story that might hint at what happened to the pioneer families. In this way, we can travel back in time to remind ourselves of the price that was paid for Texas.

Islands of Truth

(My Sources)

Alamo Traces, Thomas Ricks Lindley.

A Line in the Sand, Randy Roberts and James S. Olson.

C-Span Conference on Texas History, 2013.

Court witness interview (case 3407, Gonzales County Court).

Gonzales, Hope, Heartbreak, Heroes, Victoria Eberle Frenzel.

The Handbook of Texas online, http://www.tshaonline.org/handbook/online/.

Historical Marker 5089000347, Columbus, Texas.

Historical Marker 5177002215, Gonzales, Texas.

The History of the German Settlements in Texas 1831–1861, Rudolph Leopold Biesele.

The Indians of Texas, W.W. Newcomb, Jr.

Journey to Texas in 1833, Detlef Dunt.

Lone Star, Stephen L. Hardin.

Memoirs of George Washington Davis, family papers, Gonzales Archives.

Personal Papers, Miles S. Bennet, Gonzales Archives.

Personal Papers, Roberta Taylor, Gonzales Archives.

The Raven, Marquis James.

Santa Anna of Mexico, Will Fowler.

Stephen F. Austin, Empresario of Texas, Gregg Cantrell.

Texas Tears and Texas Sunshine, Edited by Jo Ella Powell Exley.

Texian Iliad, Stephen L. Hardin.

Women and the Texas Revolution, Mary L. Scheer.

Acknowledgments

This writing project would not have been completed without the kind support of my cousins Steven and Sandra Biersdorfer, my aunt Carole, and my husband John.

The hands-on team of editor Lillie Ammann, artist Aundrea Hernandez, and layout specialist Jan McClintock deserve my most humble appreciation.

About the Author

Betsy Wagner is a native Texan. She retired from public education in Texas after a career that also took her to schools in Louisiana, Hawaii, and Germany. She became interested in her family history after a discussion with her cousin, Steven, at a reunion. After years of research, Betsy created a story blending historical and fictional characters with events drawn from early Texas times. Today she lives with her husband in San Antonio, where she enjoys visiting with her son.

Made in the USA
Monee, IL
28 December 2019

19606581R00132